Welcome to Litorel

The Mighty Ven Devar

Quinton A. Foote

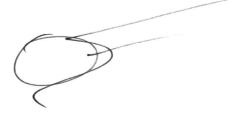

qitupproductions.com

Copyright © <2022> <Quinton A. Foote>

All rights reserved.

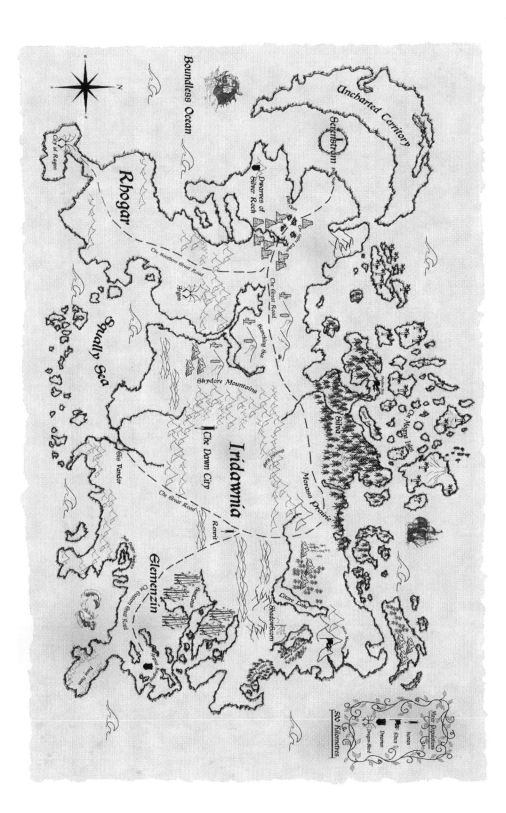

Map of Litore
Table of Contents... 1
1: The Hunters... 3
2: Silva... 9
3: Kintar and Kyst... 20
4: A Journey's End... 34
5: is a Journey's Beginning... 46
6: Dark Tidings... 66
7: Adventure Awaits... 72
8: A New Pack... 79
9: Evil in the Night... 85
10: The Right Thing... 94
11: A World Away... 100
12: Push Through... 107
13: Fresh Air... 119
14: Betrayal Grows in Trust... 126
15: The Hunted... 134
16: Belonging... 144
17: Revenge... 151
18: Ven Devar... 157

CHAPTER ONE
The Hunters

Ven Devar would often lay with his feet dangling over a cliff edge, head resting in the thick grass, dreaming of far-off places. In his 33 short years, this Kyst Elf had never found a sense of belonging among the other Kyst Elves in Silva. He was tall and slender with tightly corded muscles, toned by deep-sea diving and scaling trees that truly brushed the sky. His dark green hair swept past his pointed ears. His skin was the colour of rain clouds or an angry ocean, both complementing his ability to camouflage in the ocean and forest alike. The Kyst called the rugged coastlines and lush rainforests of Litore their home, adapting to it with grace. The citizens of Silva built their homes high above the threats of the forest floor in gigantic cedar trees.

The Kyst, like all Elves of Litore, were direct descendants of gods long past. They would accomplish much in their millennia of life. And yet so far, little of it interested Ven. His people were Sages and Hunters. They studied the forest and ocean, subsequently writing down their findings, or went fishing and hunting for their people. Tradition and perfection ruled all here, and though he valued both, Ven was at his apex when he could use his creative genius. He outperformed most, simply for his ability to look beyond the ordinary.

He was, more than once, accused of spoiling a week-long hunt for refusing to kill the animal. He could never find the words to explain it, but he always felt as though he had made a deep connection with the prey. When he got close to the kill, he always felt hunted and feared for his own life. This would only further annoy his fellow Hunters as it was widely accepted that the orphan Kyst, known as Ven Devar, was the most talented hunter in all of Silva. In truth, Ven was nearing the end of another expedition and had briefly forgotten where he was.

"Whimpering... do you hear it?" whispered Qiri, who lay on his belly next to Ven in a more focused manner. Ven slowly rolled onto his stomach and crawled the short distance to his companion. He closed off his other senses, opening his mind to the sounds around him. Wind, orchestrating tall grass, whipped through the trees. Crashing waves relentlessly struck the rock before being dragged back into the ocean. He focused through the SeaRaven's cawing, then the chitters and chirps of woodland creatures. Ven's senses were unparalleled in nature, and he quickly heard the occasional pained exhalation from a beast he could tell was a Bull Elk deeper into the woods.

"Sounds injured." Ven's tone betrayed the restful look on his face.

"If we venture off, I fear we may spoil our entire week's tracking of these PumaSheep," replied Qiri evenly. He was over a decade older than Ven, but he truly valued the creativity.

"It wouldn't be the first time we came back empty-handed," Ven retorted.

Qiri sat up, his dark-walnut hair and forest green skin popped vividly now, he wanted it too. "True, but the folks of Silva count on us to bring the most back."

Ven also sat up, brushing back his long hair and donning his hood. The pair resembled the pinnacle of Silva's finest Kyst Hunters. Both adorned in brown wool cloaks with baggy sleeves tucked neatly under their bracers. The finery of Ven's cloak was bolstered by an embroidered gold leaf pattern along the edges.

"We will find a way to make up for it," Ven suggested. "We can fish tomorrow and easily bring back a boat full if we lose the trail today." He was already quietly moving through the grass toward the whimpering. Qiri could only muster a smirk for Ven's ease of breaking the rules, so he cautiously followed behind.

As the pair walked farther into the gargantuan cedar trees and wide-sprouting ferns, the bellow of a beast emanated louder. Soon, Ven found a thick trail of blood. He waved for Qiri to keep up as he increased his speed. He felt his heart pounding and a sense of pain wash over his body. He focused through it as he climbed over a fallen tree to find a wounded Elk laying in a boggy patch of dirt. The tree was nearly nine metres off the ground; the two hunters pausing on the lip of it. Qiri stood up and knocked an arrow into his longbow. Ven arose and put out a hand to stay his shot.

"I'll do it. I want a closer look." Ven scaled down the belly of the massive fallen tree and landed firmly in soft, upturned dirt. His heart raced quicker with each footstep and with every haunting exhalation of pain from the beautiful animal. Ven walked up to the Elk laying on its side, breathing heavily and with difficulty. A single arrow shaft emerged from behind its elbow, most likely striking the beast's lungs. Judging by the amount of blood that soaked its entire side, Ven could tell the majestic animal had been suffering this fate for at least two days. Much of the flesh surrounding the wound had begun to fester, spoiling the use of its meat.

Ven pulled out his short-sword and said a quick but meaningful prayer to Āina, God of Forests, for the safe journey of this soul from our realm to the next. He wasted no time in plummeting his sword into the Bull Elk's heart, ending the torment. He felt his own heart skip a beat when the sword passed through the beast's. But then the anxiety washed over the Kyst as quickly as it came, and familiar anger replaced it.

Ven yanked on the arrow shaft and cleaned it off with a bit of water from his canteen. As he studied the craftsmanship of the arrowhead and fletching, he was interrupted by his companion.

"Need me to come down or can we get a move on?"

Ven put the arrow in his own quiver and scaled the fallen tree again, catching up to Qiri, who had already gone to pick up their last trail.

Night had fallen and the accomplished duo of hunters sat on a beach near a small fishing boat, with no rewards. Qiri added sticks to a fire that was cooking fish on hot rocks.

Ven was nestled up against a sand dune that butted against the forest floor, his large cloak sheltering him. He sat very still, staring at the arrow he had taken from the Elk. The older Kyst tucked into his meal and noticed a familiar look on Ven's face.

"Why did you keep it?" asked Qiri impassively between bites. Devar kept his eyes on the arrow.

"I know who did it. When I see him, he'll know the pain of that Elk."

Qiri raised his eyebrow but continued eating. After another few moments of heavy silence, Qiri inquired about the owner of the arrow.

"Who is the hunter responsible then?"

Ven looked to Qiri and remained silent before returning his gaze.

"Well, you can't kill whoever it was for what they did. And you would be nothing but a child for thinking otherwise."

Ven pulled his hood tight and went into a night of meditative sleep. "You must learn to control your feelings, Ven, for everyone's sake," muttered Qiri, although he wasn't sure Ven was even listening.

Ven retrieved himself from his meditative state; it was so easy to slip in and out of a sleep that offered proper rest. He awoke to find Qiri sailing a small boat some distance offshore, the full light of day not yet on the horizon. He immediately felt a pang of guilt for sleeping, since it was largely his fault they had missed out on the PumaSheep. He took off his leather chest armour and boots, readied his trident, and walked comfortably into the ocean. He loved being underwater; the way the current bounced against his eardrum made it seem like the whole world had faded away. The fish swam without care and always looked content. Often Ven would find peaceful meditation underwater, in some safe nook along the seafloor, becoming one with the ocean and its surroundings.

By the end of the day, they had caught two dozen salmon and three baskets of shellfish to bring back. All in all, what they had caught by day's end would average what most hunting parties would catch over the whole expedition.

That evening, the duo found themselves in the elegantly carved Hunter's Hall that perched precariously among the many enormous sprouting trunks of an Arbutus tree. It sat proudly near the centre of Silva, with two massive statues of Kyst Hunters looking down on all those who entered. After they had dropped off their game, Qiri couldn't get a word in before Ven stormed off to find whoever injured the Elk.

Ven often thought he had the patience for too much in life, but he could never let the laziness and cruelty of half-killing an animal go unpunished. The hunters in the corridors all collectively turned to watch Ven clutching a blood-stained arrow as he stormed his way to the common room. It agitated him further knowing the only reason they were staring, was because of his reputation, which he despised in and of itself.

Soon, the doors to the common room were flung open, revealing a large, vaulted hall made from ancient mahogany. The walls were lined with several crackling fireplaces, bookshelves, tactical maps, and various spots of comfort. It was customary for the hunters to wear their full gear inside the hall, so Ven was confident he could find the quiver this arrow belonged to. Pausing in the centre of the room, he looked around intensely, breathing far heavier than he realized. Several clusters of Kyst paused to look back at him with wide eyes. An Elder named Andil arose from his comfy seat next to a fire.

"Is everything all right, Devar?" His voice sounded dry with age.

Ven spotted his target, who was awkwardly shifting behind a comrade to hide. Ven could hear his own heart pounding as he stoically approached the hunter known as Ehan. Ehan was a Kyst 400 years into his role and had recently begun causing trouble on hunts. Once Ehan knew Ven was on to him, he stood proud and taller than the approaching, smaller Kyst, easily outweighing Ven by nearly 40 kilograms. Ven shoved the bloody arrow against Ehan's leather chest armour.

"Tell everyone where you left this." He said loudly enough for the whole room to hear.

"I seem to not remember?" Ehan replied, feigning ignorance.

Ven's eyes ignited at the blatant denial.

"Then let me remind you." Ven dropped low, spinning on his heel before plunging the arrow deep into the side of Ehan's thigh. Ehan let out a sharp yelp of pain. Qiri walked in just in time to hear the cry. Ven took it a step further when he continued the spin, leading with his free foot to kick Ehan's feet out from under him, causing the exceptionally large Kyst to connect hard with the solid floor. Before anyone could react, Ven was on top of Ehan, holding a dagger to his throat, seeing all red. The Elder, Andil, filled the room with an unnaturally booming voice.

"What is the meaning of this, Ven Devar!"

Qiri dropped his head to the side in disappointment.

"Ehan decided to put an arrow through the lung of a Bull Elk on his hunt but couldn't be bothered to finish what he started," Ven explained. "If I am not mistaken, Elder Andil, it was you who passed a law 900 years ago, making such acts punishable by death."

Ehan's face filled with genuine terror as he looked into the eyes of a fellow hunter about to execute his prey. All the other Kyst in the room might as well have been ghosts, for they were silent and still. Ven's tired voice was replaced by a booming one.

"Yes, but that judgement is not for you to decide nor carry out, Mighty Ven Devar. Now release him," Andil replied dryly. Ven let go of a whimpering Ehan, tucked his dagger back into one of the many sheaths on his raiment, and stormed out of the common room. Qiri tried to talk to his friend but Ven simply pushed past him.

CHAPTER TWO

Silva

The melodic screeching of the SeaRavens above paired synonymously with the colossal crashing waves below. It was times like this that I thought myself fortunate to live in Silva, another creature existing in harmony with the Ocean, and great rainforests. The crisp autumn rain and ocean spray never left me at a loss for nostalgia. Yet all of this was only enough to pull me away from thoughts of other places for short periods of time. New lands filled with history, adventure and people of intrigue, was what my heart desired. If I'm scolded one more time for refusing an outdated tradition, I just may jump off this cliff and swim to a distant land; never to look back. If I did go away from this place, would I even want to look back? Silva is my home if I ever had one, but I am as familiar with family as I am with death. It has always been me and the wild. What unknown destinations or friends would I stumble upon. Or perhaps my destiny truly does lie as nothing more than a hunter of Silva. Would that be so bad? I know not the answer and so perhaps that is why I'm afraid.

-Ven Devar

Night had taken over and Ven was laying in the thick grass with his legs dangling over a seaside cliff. Wearing the traditional clothes of Silva he was wrapped up warmly in his cloak. Billions of stars filled the sky offering a breathtaking vista, yet the three moons, set against the sparkling backdrop, always grabbed the eye with their distinct and up-close beauty. Hours had passed before he opened his opalescent green eyes when a raindrop struck him between the brow. Raising his torso and wiggling his toes over thin air, Ven gripped the edge of the cliff and slightly rocked back and forth. Staring at the dangerously enticing drop, wishing he had the courage to take the leap. Eventually letting out a sigh he rolled onto his back and sprang up to his feet. He tilted his head as a screech from a SeaRaven caught his ear. It had occurred to him more than once that a particular SeaRaven had been following him of late.

"Leave me alone, bird." He muttered through a yawn and stretch. From deep in the forest came an ear-piercing scream. Ven's skin recoiled, his eyes widened and before he had time to process the cry, he felt his feet sprinting towards the distressed. Just as he began to think he had lost the trail another shriek came from close by.

A slender figure with a large, billowing, and tattered cloak stood with her back against a tree that was three metres wide before rounding off. Surrounding the cloaked figure was a pack of hungry wolves. They snarled their bone pulverizing teeth and snapped at the air with malevolence. The alpha was closing in and blended flawlessly with the night. The beast's fur was mostly black but had white spots that looked like stars on the clearest night.

Ven soon found the figure surrounded and felt his stomach meet his feet. It wasn't a rare thing for hunters to encounter packs of wolves and for that reason, he was aware that a single wolf was capable of killing a beast much larger than itself. A victim to one of these pack attacks might find their legs numbed as the wolves bite away at the ankles and thighs to immobilize the creature. Then the hot breath of a wide jaw, filled with razor-sharp fangs enshrouding your face, before snapping shut, delivering you into eternal darkness

As the terrified figure was about to let out another scream of desperation, a whistle from behind the wolves sounded out. Ven, with his shins planted to the earth and hands in his lap, maintained direct eye contact with the alpha. A series of heart-pounding growls emanated from the pack of glowing wolf eyes that now turned their collective gaze away from the figure towards the Kyst Hunter.

The alpha moved with intent towards him. The wolf remained low, teeth bared and hackles taught. Ven dared not blink. He had no idea what he was doing, but he did recognize this black and white wolf. He had seen it on more than one occasion and even had a similar stand-off the previous winter. Back then, Ven had struck a stag low with a single arrow through both eyes. The alpha wolf challenged him for the kill, however, he understood at the time that the wolf just needed to feed his pack. Ven had left the Stag for the alpha to drag away. Now, this wolf stood just under two metres tall on all fours. Ven could only guess he was nearly 226 kilograms heavy, which is to say nearly double since their last encounter.

Edging forward, the alpha now stood only centimetres away from Ven's shimmering eyes. He stayed as still as a statue, his muscles aching from the stiffness of only a few short moments of tense immobility. The eyes of the hooded figure slipped through the cowl to reveal a vibrant grey stare from a young and starkly pale woman. Eyes that looked on in amazement as the alpha wolf slowly nuzzled his forehead against the Kyst's. Ven slowly raised one hand to place on the thick mane of the majestic beast. By the time the alpha had pulled his fury head back to look Ven in the eyes, all the other wolves had left. Ven slowly rose to his feet when he heard a faint question.

"Who are you?" whispered the cloaked figure. Ven knew people rarely, if ever, got lost and wandered into the Great Northern Rainforest.

"A local, which you are not. What are you doing out here?"

The cloaked figure took a few steps closer to Ven and removed her hood. It was a woman with ghostly white skin, bright grey eyes, and black hair that at the ends, appeared as if misted away into shadow. Ven was severely taken aback by the awe of her. She moved with such precision and intent, almost floating in her steps.

"I was on a convoy heading South to Rhogar when we were attacked by monsters. I'm the only survivor."

"How close by?" He responded evenly.

The Woman looked at him sorrowfully. "I don't know, I just ran and kept running for days." She collapsed to her knees from exhaustion. "I thought I was going to be torn to shreds before you showed up. I don't know what I'm doing out here. Or where here is."

Ven knelt beside her. "My people can help you." When the silence and doubt continued he thought it a good idea to introduce himself. "I'm Ven Devar, of Silva. Do you know it?" he asked with a comforting smile. She looked back at him with her bright eyes. "I do. I'm Scáth."

Ven offered her his hand and she took it with a brief pause of hesitation. Ven hurriedly led them towards Silva.

"Where do you hail from Scáth?"

"A small kingdom near the Moon Mountains." She responded kindly, but Ven couldn't help but notice she wasn't keen to elaborate. After walking for roughly thirty minutes through large, overgrown flora, they halted.

"Well, we're here, just in time too! I think I hear a herd of PumaSheep trailing us."

Scáth raised a brow. "PumaSheep?"

"The cutest, softest, and the deadliest creature you'll find in the Great Northern Rainforest. Worry not though." Ven gave three short whistles. It reminded Scáth of a songbird she had heard while rushing through the forest the day before. She took a surprised step back as a rope ladder fell from above and unfurled gently at their feet.

Ven motioned to the ladder. "After you, milady."

"This is the only way up?" She asked nervously.

Ven shrugged. "Unfortunately, but it is well worth it once you are there."

Scáth grasped the first rung and began to climb. Ven paused to have another look at the dim forest floor. The only light offered was bioluminescent flora, fungi, and the occasional glowing animal. As he grabbed the first rung, an owl gave three hoots and the ladder began to retract, acting like a rudimentary elevator system. The hunter held tight and slowly watched the forest floor shrink and disappear beneath him as he entered the canopy line. Much to his delight, he spotted Scáth standing at the landing platform, awestruck by the city before her.

Silva was built in the canopy of one massive forest that surrounded much of Litore's northern coastlines. Hundreds of elegantly carved wood houses protrude from, and intrude into, the massive Cedar trunks. A harmonious relationship between craft and nature. The canopy was open and at this height, was witness to a night sky filled with colourful stars. This elegant settlement was interlinked by sturdy bridges marked up and down with more bioluminescent flora and fungi. Three Kyst hunters who raised the ladder approached the duo. Ven immediately recognized them, as Silva had a population of nearly five thousand. He also recognized an immediate hostility and found himself protective of the woman.

A Kyst named Rexous led the approaching group. He was similar to Ven in many ways and the two had an infamous rivalry. Rexous was steeped in tradition and was the most irritating kind of perfectionist. These two hunters were often at odds with each other as Ven usually outperformed Rexous on most hunts.

"Grab her." Rexous motioned towards Scáth.

Ven wasted no time stepping between Scáth and the Hunter Guards. "She's under my protection."

The two Kyst hunters stopped abruptly, neither of them wishing to fight against Ven, not even when they outnumbered him.

"You know the rule about outsiders. She meets the queen and then she can walk free." The Kyst were protective to a fault. There were many races in Litore, and more than not were nightmarish, blood-hungry savages. Many fell races were killers of the vilest kind. When one of these races went to work they always made sure that the settlement wasn't left standing to raid again. Scáth looked at Ven with doubt.

"So your soldiers can stay here guarding the ladder and the three of us can go see the queen," Ven said as if it was already agreed. A scowl crossed Rexous' face as he reluctantly ordered his Elves to stay beside the ladder. Ven looked to Scáth and offered a wink. He was glad to see her posture relax as they followed Rexous over the bridges and around ornate buildings with wide helical attached walkways.

"I wish not to bother or cause strife for your people," Scáth said honestly.

"If we turned away those in need of a helping hand, we'd be no better than a pack of pillaging Kintar," he answered with a wry smile.

"You are kind, Ven Devar. Tell me about your home. I have heard of Kyst Elves but never enjoyed the pleasure of experiencing their culture."

Ven was eager to explain. "This forest pre-dates the first age. Truthfully by the time Silva has come and gone, it will only have been a short time in the existence of this forest. We've learned the best ways to co-exist with the life around us. Never to take more than we need, and give back when you can. In fact, it's that way of thinking, which might have saved you tonight. I had given that same wolf a stag I struck low last winter."

Scáth was mesmerized to hear Ven speak of the Forest with such reverence as if it were a living, breathing creature to communicate with, just as easily as they were doing now. She listened eagerly as he explained the many legends and lore of this place.

"The Kyst were driven to the coasts of Litore at the end of the first age by monsters and wicked folk. Hardier and more adaptable races like the Dwarves, Humans or other Elves remained inland. From there we grew to live among the trees and hunt the forest and sea for survival. So that leads us to an age-old tradition of meeting any and all outsiders before allowing them to stay in our settlement." Ven for some reason felt embarrassed explaining all this to her. Outsiders were few indeed but not all that uncommon in Silva. Surely though not many residents had outsiders they called 'friends'.

"It's okay." She replied softly. "I am familiar with such securities from my own home."

He looked to her, hopeful that she would continue but again, she did not elaborate. Just as the question was about to leave his lips, Rexous interrupted.

"We're here" he noted, with a sense of relief in his voice. Ven and Scáth stood shortly behind Rex as he motioned for the doors to be opened. The two massive doors, intricately carved with the history of the Silva people, swung inwards. It revealed a Great Hall, unlike Scáth had ever imagined. Vines and bushes grew from the walls. Bioluminescent fungi clung to the dark ceilings, appearing as scattered starlight from the floor. Every piece of furniture looked as though it took an Elf's lifetime to craft. Motionless but imposing, heavily armoured guards stood at four-metre intervals along each wall, guarding the throne in which a particularly resplendent Kyst woman sat. After walking a short distance from the door towards the throne, a melodic voice echoed through the hall.

"My Son, who have you brought to me?"

Rexous immediately gave way to a low bow before rising and proudly stating. "Mother, I found Ven trying to sneak in an outsider." Ven made a point of dramatically rolling his eyes. The queen, from her throne of ever weaving roots, and vines with autumn-coloured leaves, turned her heavy gaze upon him. He took a few steps forward and gave a no less respectful bow.

"My queen, I offer no such offence. I found this woman lost and alone within our borders past dusk, nearly set upon by a pack of wolves. It is our way to offer aid to those in true need, is it not?" The magnificent queen held her silence for longer than expected, looking down upon Scáth with an intense stare.

"Indeed it is, Ven Devar. Will your guest not introduce herself?"

Scáth took a graceful step forward and offered a fanciful bow. "Pardon me, Your Majesty. I am Scáth ShadowScorn. Your warrior speaks the truth, I owe him my life." Her hair fell forwards, giving the queen a better view of Scáth's shadowy locks misting away like the spray at the basin of a waterfall. The queen arose from her throne. Much to Scáth's surprise, she was quite tall, far taller than the males around her.

"What is a ShadowScorn doing in our forest?" Scáth felt a familiar sense of prejudice. Ven and Rexous looked to each other only to see if the other knew who or what a ShadowScorn was. They both quickly looked away when each spotted the other sharing the same thought. A worried look crossed Scáth's face.

"I had been ripped away from home. They were transporting me to Serenstrom. There I would be auctioned off for the pleasure of some homicidal or religious monster. A common fate for many of my people I'm afraid. I managed to escape, having wandered for days before Ven Devar found me."

"So what would you have me do, Scáth?"

Scáth remained quiet, eyes to the floor. Ven saw an opportunity to speak the truth.

"I'd have you grant her respite, my queen. Then I would have you send a troop of our finest hunters to see her safely home." Ven looked to Scáth with hopeful anticipation. Rex stared at him fiercely. The queen raised a brow in Ven's direction before he continued to speak. "I have only ever looked upon you with admiration. So I would have you, my queen, do what you know is right."

"How dare you!" Snapped Rexous but his Mother was swift to stay his emotions.

"Very well, I cannot as of yet promise all that you seek. However, until I have reached a decision, she may stay if you're willing to host."

Scáth was stunned by how Ven spoke to his queen on her behalf. She barely knew anything about this Kyst hunter and yet he appeared to be taking great risks for her. She wondered what was more terrifying for him; approaching a pack of hungry wolves or speaking against his Ruler.

Ven was a little surprised by everything that had just transpired. Normally, meeting a guest is a formality. He wondered why the queen would need to think on it, surely Scáth was no threat. Granted he had never seen anyone like her but assumed from the conversation that her race had something to do with the 'ShadowScorn'. It also occurred to him that Scáth's story had changed slightly since their first encounter.

"Thank you, my queen. I will make sure she keeps to our ways and causes no botherations."

Ven gave a low bow and Scáth quickly followed suit. They turned and made their way for the exit. The pale-skinned woman who walked without a sound, made her exit. She looked once more to the mesmerizing star-light fungi in the ceiling. As they walked through Silva, she looked to Ven and then to the folk around her. Much to her bewilderment, they spent more time looking at him with a sense of respect than they did staring at her. The ShadowScorn were a race that manifested into existence overnight, descending from a village of various races coming into contact with a shadow deity. They first graced Litore's land only a thousand years ago, and had ever since been the targets of evil and insecure beings.

"Are you hungry?" Ven's voice retrieved Scáth from her thoughts.

"Yes!" She exclaimed excitedly. Despite everything that had transpired in the previous few days, food was all but in the background of her mind.

"Great, one moment then." Ven entered a small and warmly glowing tavern.

She paused to survey her surroundings when the sound of rushing water caught her ear. Scáth considered it was possible that Silva had rivers or waterfalls that flowed below. She walked a short distance to where the canopy had taken cover again; the world darkening around her, aside from the glowing fungi that lined the large wooden paths. Around a bend and past a few homes, she began to feel mist accumulating upon her porcelain skin. The sound of rushing water grew louder. She rubbed her slender fingers across her cheek, and as the water pooled on her fingertips and became agitated, it glowed slightly.

Ven spotted Scáth a moment after she had wandered away. He was holding two bowls of a delectable Kyst soup. He kept his distance and allowed her this moment of discovery in peace. She walked a little further and finally spotted it. A raging waterfall of bright cyan poured from a natural tunnel in the rock wall. In awe of the natural beauty around her, she watched the vibrant water gushing through Silva and down to the forest floor, where it undoubtedly continued flowing to the ocean. Scáth looked over her shoulder and spotted her host sitting on a bench nearby, holding up a bowl in her direction. She eagerly made her way to join him on the bench but was held up for a moment as two Kyst townsfolk paid their respects to Ven, thanking him for a wonderful supply of food. After they left, Scáth took her spot beside him.

He handed her the bowl. "Best soup in Silva" he said, as he plunged a spoonful into his mouth. Scáth looked at it and thought it was more of a stew than soup but was happy nonetheless. She took a bite and felt her taste buds explode in joy.

"Why does everyone get so excited when you pass?" she asked between bites "I mean clearly, Rexous is the Prince." Ven chuckled at the remark.

"Well, I'm a hunter. I was top of my class and have continued to yield the best results out of any other hunter in our history. It's tradition to treat us with reverence and sanctity. There was also an incident with an Ice Demon some years past, but that tale is for another time. Though, if I am to be honest, I hate the renown." Ven had never been ego-driven, which was uncommon among the other hunters.

"Don't like the attention?"

"Truthfully, I don't like being reminded of how easy killing comes to me." Ven continued to eat. The thought had crossed his mind prior but surely it was the first time he had spoken those words aloud. Scáth liked that though. It proved an air of sensitivity and innocence in the Elf, and it was the most she had learned about him thus far.

After they devoured their meal and Ven had allowed Scáth to fully take in the view, they headed for his home. Everything was put to use in Silva; nothing was ever wasted by the Kyst. Ven had opened the door to his home before Scáth had even realized that there was an entrance on the face of the tree. He walked in and she entered a moment later. It was quaint and humble. He immediately went to light a fire in the hearth. It consisted of two rooms and Scáth noted only one bed.

"Where might I find rest tonight, Ven?" she asked innocently. Ven looked around. He didn't have guests over. Ever.

"Well, the other room is an armoury. Only the one bed, so I will make sure you have everything you need and go back down to the forest floor for the night." He thought it to be a nice idea actually. He barely spent any time in his home anyhow. He was always happier sleeping in the wild and living in the elements.

"Surely I cannot put you out of your own home on top of all you have done for me."

"The night is near half over milady, I would gladly spend the remaining hours in the place I am happiest. And besides, this way I can bring you breakfast." Ven was all but insistent. "Please take your time to get comfortable. I will be in my armoury for a moment before leaving you to some much-needed peace."

Scáth uttered a quiet response. "Okay."

Ven walked into his favourite room and shut the heavy door behind him, leaving Scáth in the space alone.

She was uncomfortable around such kindness as it was a foreign concept to her regular life. She looked at the many rugs, blankets, and furs laying around; draped across chairs, folded into thick piles. It was a cozy and warm home, which was something she had not had for some time. She stood by the hearth for warmth and spotted a gold medallion displayed atop a shelf. Shining in the orange-glow of the fire, it caught her attention, not only for its beauty, but also that it happened to be the only metal item in the room. She fingered a small clasp on one side and opened it. She was surprised to see what was inside.

The armoury was smaller than the main room but held all of his gear. Several bows, short swords, tridents, and daggers hung on the wall. They were of the finest Elven Craft in Litore. For some traditions truly did pay off, this time in the form of the greatest Kyst blacksmiths in all the land. In the center of the room hung an admirable leather suit of armour, intricately weaved together to give the wearer optimal flexibility and strength. A leather breastplate formed to the shape his muscular torso. Attached to it were several sheaths for daggers and a scabbard above the tailbone for a short-sword. After dawning his famous Armour of Silva, he clipped his trident to a belt around his hip. He then put on his large dark brown cloak made from the soft and warm wool of a PumaSheep. He donned his hood and strapped a large quiver of silver-tipped arrows to his back and slung a longbow around his shoulder. At that point, it occurred to Ven for whatever reason, that most of his greatest adventures and stories started in this very room. He enjoyed a look around the armoury before heading into the living room. When he opened the door he spotted Scáth next to the fire studying his locket. When she heard him enter she put the open locket down, facing him.

"Is this your Father?" Scáth said with genuine sincerity. Ven walked over, closed it, and put it around his neck.

"No." He replied dryly before tucking it under his many layers. Scáth looked down, slightly ashamed by her intrusive question.

Ven looked at her large, vibrant, alluring eyes and felt his heart skip a beat. Scáth looked back at him, in his fine armour and dark-green hair swept back, and felt the sudden urge to ask him to stay the night. Before she mustered the courage however, Ven walked to the front door and paused before leaving.

"Good night, milady." He closed the door behind him and Scáth found herself alone with nothing but the sound of crackling embers. She threw another log into the fire and sat on the edge of her bed, letting out a great sigh.

CHAPTER THREE

Kintar and Kyst

Ven breathed deeply, filling his lungs with fresh air, contemplating his next step. He thought some company might do him well. His status in Silva didn't make having friends easy, however. Much rivalry or jealousy would arise from the other hunters, but he did have one dear friend who was much more like a brother. So he started off only a short distance from his own home. His good friend Vakar was not a Hunter of Silva but a Sage. The sages were obsessed with nature, philosophy, history, and magic. Nearly twenty years ago, Vakar had first approached Ven seeking help in gathering herbs and ingredients from the forest floor. Needless to say, a lifelong friendship had been forged that day, as they shared a brush with death when they happened upon a scouting party of Kintar. It was now the dead of night but that didn't stop Ven from aggressively banging on Vakar's door. He might have considered being quieter but he noticed a bright light from one of the windows. Vakar was quick to swing his door open.

"Excuse me Ven Devar, but you don't catch me banging on your door at this unholy hour." Vakar was trying his hardest to act annoyed.

"You woke me up this time just last week when you ran out of hemlock," Ven replied flatly.

Vakar appeared perplexed. "Yes." Ven pushed past him and sat down at the table.

"Out on a hunt, dear friend?" Vakar asked curiously.

"Was just hoping to take a stroll and share some conversation. Figured I'd be prepared for what lurks in the night if need be." Ven fingered a strange item on the tabletop that was some amalgamation of weaved metal and wood.

Vakar needed only one look at his hunter companion to understand something was wrong.

"Of course. Let me get ready." the sage replied, as he hurried into his laboratory leaving the door open.

"What are you doing up this late, Vakar?" queried Ven.

"Brought home some books about the topic you requested. Rest alludes me of late, so figured I'd make use of the time."

Ven nodded to himself. "Any progress?"

Vakar walked back into the room, fully dressed in long heavy robes, with a satchel stuffed with various spell components and books. He walked over to Ven and put a hand on his shoulder.

"There are a lot of Kyst Elves and settlements like ours living in Litore. I promise I will find your birthplace, but it will take time." Vakar answered evenly. Ven gave a half-hearted smile before rising from his chair.

Instead of taking one of the ladders, they decided to descend via Vakar's tree. All Kyst Elves learned to scale trees, swim, and walk at the same time. The average Kyst could free-dive up to 300 metres for nearly an hour on a single breath, or climb a kilometre tall tree as fast as it would take to run it.

It was not long before Ven and Vakar were sitting at the mouth of a river that trickled into the ocean, cooking fish and a rabbit over a warm fire. The horizon was beginning to regain its colour as the sun slowly neared the eastern skyline.

"I saw the queen last night." Ven blurted out between bites. Vakar wasn't surprised by that, but curious.

"Let me guess, her Highness wanted to congratulate you on another successful Hunt?" Vakar teased, but Ven remained serious.

"I found a woman in the forest, mere seconds away from being devoured by a pack of wolves." Ven struggled to remember the details as to why the wolves actually left. "I managed to scare them off. She was okay, thankfully. But she's different, you know?" Ven looked up to his friend, who stared back, eagerly awaiting the rest of his story. "She's-"

Vakar finished Ven's thought. "-Beautiful, unlike anything you've ever dreamt of."

Ven blushed. "Not exactly. She appears as if made from shadow more than flesh.

"Interesting. Well, where is she? The queen let her stay, yes?" Vakar felt agitated on his friends' behalf.

"Yes, yes. My reputation is what earned Scáth her stay, I believe. She's currently in my home."

Vakar let out a hardy laugh. "Which is why we are here is it not, Ven Devar?"

Ven ignored him. Vakar and the Kyst Hunter, Qiri had been madly in love since childhood. They planned on getting married and moving in together this winter. Ven pulled off a white chunk of fish in an attempt to hide his flustered emotions from Vakar.

"The only thing on Litore that could displace the Mighty Ven Devar from his own quarters, is a beautiful girl... what does the queen plan to do with her?" Vakar asked optimistically.

Ven shrugged. "We go back to see her in the morning."

Vakar looked up to the fading stars. "Only a few hours before sunrise. Close your eyes, my friend. I will keep the fire warm and read one of those books I mentioned." Ven hadn't rested properly for almost three days, which wasn't all that uncommon but he was feeling particularly weary. If he didn't have to meet the queen and have his wits honed in a few hours he would have refused.

"Thank you," Ven muttered already settling in for a restful trance. He sat cross-legged with his palms facing the sky, closed his green eyes and drifted fast away.

Vakar stirred the embers, throwing another log into the fire and settling in with a book. He stared at his dear friend and adopted brother for a long while. Vakar knew him better than any soul in Silva, in Litore for that matter. For that reason, he took pride in being there for him when Ven needed it. Vakar was a genius, he excelled as an acolyte and made the rank of Sage as one of the youngest Kyst in Silva history. Unfortunately for the pair, this meant he was not nearly as adept in the Wild. Vakar pulled out a pipe and began to fill it with various exotic weeds. Ven remained meditating, still as stone.

Behind them, roughly 20 metres, stood four Kintar hiding among the bushes. The Kintar were beastly Elves, once akin to the Kyst, but refused their new way of life upon arriving in the Great Northern Rainforest all those millennia ago. From there, the Kintar broke off as their own kind, embracing life as raiders and barbarians. They worshiped Lokor, god of battle. Similar in appearance to the Kyst, evolution had molded them into broader stronger Elves. Unlike their cousins, they wore ragged furs with minimal armour as they were far larger and packed with far more muscle than the average Kyst. They also carried crude weapons, forged from the bones of their fallen foe. Speaking in their own guttural language similar to Kystin, the smallest Kintar, clad in throwing knives, spoke to its leader. A Kintar much larger than the rest who was covered from his bald head to bare toes in tattoos.

"That's the hunter, Ven Devar. This will make Uthul's attack much easier than planned." said the small one, with a sickening snicker.

"Who's the robed Elf?" murmured the tattooed Kintar.

"A sage weakling." answered another from the Scouting party.

The tattooed Kintar slowly nodded to his little companion. The little Kintar pulled out one of the many knives strapped to his shoulder and, with an evil grin, lined it up with Ven's head. He threw with all his might and the knife went spinning towards the hunter. An unpredictable gust of wind dropped the dagger barely but enough to lodge the dagger into Ven's quiver, rather than his skull.

Vakar's eyes widened. Ven's eyes didn't even open before he had sprung into action. In one swift motion, he rolled to the side, pulled an arrow from his quiver with his longbow in hand. He came back up to a kneeling stance and loosed an arrow in the exact direction the knife came from. He never saw a target but knew he connected when he heard a gurgled scream. The arrow had traveled through the small Kintar's mouth, to where it now protruded out the back of his head. Vakar jumped to his feet, preparing the incantations of a powerful spell.

The tell-tale sign of a Kintar attack was heard as a roar echoed through the forest, then three Raiders erupted from the tree line. Before one of the foul beasts had even raised his weapon high, Ven sent an arrow forthwith through his heart. Vakar let a burst of red energy pulse from his hand, incinerating the other Kintar. The Tattooed behemoth hit Vakar once under the chin, sending the sage flying headlong into the river.

Ven sent another arrow his way catching him in the shoulder. The menacing Kintar bellowed loudly and sprinted with his spiked club poised right for the Kyst's face. The Kintar swung hard causing Ven to drop his bow and roll to the side. He grabbed the knife protruding from his quiver and underhand threw it at the tattooed thigh. The Kintar seemed unfazed by the pain, and instead stared at the Elf with rage-filled eyes.

Ven then pulled his elegant short-sword from its sheath. He glanced across at his robed friend who was slowly but surely making his way to the river's edge. Ven crouched low in a defensive stance and taunted his enemy to attack. The Raider sprinted forward swinging furiously. Ven ducked and weaved through the attacks, managing to drag his sword across the Kintar's bicep. The Kintar swung his club down from the left, forcing Ven to dodge right, straight into the Brutes awaiting free hand. Ven's eyes widened by the sudden grapple and the Kintar smashed his forehead into the hunters' nose. With blood staining Ven's vision, next thing he knew his back cracked and the wind escaped his lungs as he was flung against a tree so hard, a mass of leaves fell, blanketing him. Ven, still laying down, grabbed the dagger strapped to his chest and threw it at the Raider, skewering the freehand. The Kintar roared once more before speaking in Kystin.

"Such a shame you won't be alive to watch us hang her with her own entrails." Ven felt a wave of fear wash over him for Scáth. Any Warrior worth their title would have let the bigger opponent tire themselves before taking the offensive. But Ven learned that this Kintar was so large and excited that he would be reacting to the first hit by the time Ven was three attacks ahead. The hunter got to his feet, drew another dagger with his free hand and responded proudly.

"No one will ever harm her again." The hunter sprang at the massive Kintar, unleashing a hail of strikes from sword and dagger, both high and low. The Raider couldn't believe the speed and accuracy of this Kyst. He managed to block one out of every three cuts and jabs with his large wooden club. Even going so far as to grab the short-sword with one hand, but Ven quickly slipped and sliced it from his grasp. The hunter felt his adrenaline surge every time his blade opened flesh.

The Kintar kicked and swung in defence but Ven was already somewhere else. He saw his moment when the sorry Kintar exposed his center. Ven shoved the dagger into his belly, kicked off with his right foot, spinning around on his left heel and dragging the blade all the way around to his spine. The Kintar reacted violently. Ven kicked the back of his knee and dropped the beast, dragging his dagger up as his foe fell. The Kintar dropped forward, utterly lifeless. The hunter exhaled deeply and wiped the blood from his eyes.

Ven waved to his companion, Vakar, who returned the gesture and walked over, dripping wet. Ven took a moment to regain his senses. He sniffed the air a few times and caught no scent of more enemies, even with a favourable wind. What he did smell was smoke. Vakar sidled up next to the dead tattooed Kintar to search him.

"Do you smell that?" asked Ven.

"Smoke. I pulverized the one Raider," Vakar said, pointing to a pile of smouldering ash.

Ven didn't respond and sprinted off into the forest. Vakar needn't hear anything else, he trusted his friends' senses more than anyone.

They had walked nearly an hour to the river's end and now after running side by side, jumping and weaving their way through the subtropical rainforest, smoke truly began to fill the air.

"No." muttered Ven under his breath. The two friends ran even harder and soon saw the light of flames coming from Silva. Ven and Vakar looked at each other, their wide-eyes filled with dread.

"It was a Kintar Scouting party, Ven."

"We must hurry. Find Qiri and start sending everyone to the ocean." Ven ordered. Vakar wasted no time and began to climb the nearest tree. Ven ran only a short distance to the tree trunk of his home. He climbed with the grace and speed of a cougar. The smoke was thick and the muffled cries of help emanated from the canopy. Once breaching the thickest of it, he jumped onto the platform and found hundreds of Kintar storming Silva, lighting everything ablaze. Ven ducked low momentarily as a hoard of raiders passed him. He kicked open his door with sword and trident drawn to find Scáth holding a scimitar from his armoury. She looked with relief as he walked through the door and quickly but quietly closed it behind him.

"Fine choice of weapon, milady. If we make it through this, it's yours." Ven said hopefully as he peered through one of the small windows.

"What's going on out there? Who is it?" Scáth's calm demeanour intrigued Ven.

"It would appear to be a Kintar raiding army. How they got up here or why is beyond my knowledge as of yet." Ven walked over to Scáth and put a hand on her shoulder. "I promise to let no harm come to you."

She smiled and truly believed he would protect her. Or at least try. What was at the front of Scáth's mind was if she was responsible for this disaster. Horrid things kept happening since her kidnapping the months before.

"I trust you, Ven Devar." She proclaimed honestly.

Ven slowly opened the door and a giant cloud of smoke filled his home. It was growing exponentially worse with every minute. Ven caught two Kintar chasing a Mother and her Child. He quickly drew his bow, knocked it with two arrows, and fell both Kintar simultaneously. The Mother waved his way and jumped onto a tree with her Child. Ven reached behind him for Scáth, as soon as they exited the home, Ven heard a Kintar yell in their harsh native tongue.

"There she is!" Ven was rusty in their guttural language but understood their intent. Four Kintar Barbarians rushed Ven and Scáth. He sent three arrows and three arrows found their target. One Kintar took the brunt of the arrow but his minimal armour kept it from doing severe harm. Ven ran up to him, jumped, retracted his feet and kicked the Kintar, with his powerful legs, square in the chest. The Barbarian flew into a Raider trailing close behind. Ven landed on his back and was quick to his feet, plunging sword and trident into both hearts before either had a chance to stand.

He looked back to see Scáth retrieving her scimitar from the ribcage of one unlucky Raider from a different pack who thought her to be an easy target. He was relieved to see Scáth wasn't afraid to spill blood, in self-defence at least. Ven was quick to notice another troop of at least ten Raiders heading their way all shouting, "The Shadow Girl!" He didn't have much time to think but it dawned on him that bringing Scáth here could have been an error. At least considering the amount of attention she was attracting. He ran to her, grabbed her hand tightly and they both rushed away.

Their lungs heaved, working overtime to fight off the soup like smoke. The entire canopy was on fire at this point. It didn't appear as though there was a single place in Silva where you could hide from the malicious heat. Hundreds of hunters were out now, battling with a passion unlike any had felt before. This battle was for their home. Perhaps they could not see what Ven could, but he knew in his heart that Silva was lost. The town he called home whether he liked it or not would soon be ash. He never let go of Scáth, their legs pumping strenuously, coughing harder with each passing moment. He kept his short-sword at chest height ready to parry any Kintar in their path. All of a sudden Ven felt great resistance from Scáth and a subsequent "Help!"

He whipped his head around and spotted a large Barbarian grasping Scáth's other hand, with a rusty and jagged sword raised high. Scáth looked up in terror and before she knew it, a mist of blood-soaked her face as a dagger flew from Ven straight into the Raiders eye. They were off again before she could fully register what had happened.

At last, Ven spotted his dear friends Vakar and Qiri, back to back with a pile of at least fifteen dead Raiders at their feet. The hunter and sage lovers complimented each other exquisitely. Qiri and Ven spent many of their hunts together and so Vakar joked it was Ven's duty to make sure his true love always came home in one piece. Ven ran up to them as Vakar ducked, allowing Qiri to slice the throat of the last approaching Kintar. Qiri hadn't seen Ven since the Hunter's Hall.

"Glad to see you're giving these Kintar a warm welcome," Ven said vigorously. Vakar and Qiri both greeted him with relief.

Ven then looked to Scáth. "Milady, these are my dearest friends and they will protect you until I return." Amidst all the carnage and war, Vakar still managed a fanciful bow and introduced himself and his boyfriend. Vakar then raised his hand for Scáth to take.

"I promise no harm will befall you while you're with us Scáth" Said Qiri with genuine kindness. Looking at the bodies around them she truly believed it. But she didn't feel right leaving Ven's side.

"No." She responded sternly. She grasped Ven's hand tighter and looked up to him. He returned the gaze before saying,

"I must find our queen, it's not safe for you to join me." Scáth's firmness did not yield. Ven let out a small sigh and looked back at his friends. Vakar had a cheeky grin on his face, it was rare Ven ever took 'no' for an answer.

"Continue the evacuation. We will join you as soon as possible." Vakar and Qiri nodded and the group divided once more. Ven and Scáth started towards the Throne Room they had visited earlier. When they were roughly fifty metres from the entrance, Ven struggled to spot what was happening through the smoke.

"Hop on my back," He instructed Scáth with haste. The last thing she wanted was to be a hindrance after refusing to leave him so she did so willingly. Scáth wrapped her arms around his neck tightly as Ven lowered them over the side of one of the many large wooden bridges in Silva. With one iron grip holding them securely over a drop Scáth didn't want to think about, he put the other hand on the wood and began whispering to himself. Soon a door appeared from nowhere, and they slipped into the darkness.

"A secret passage for the queen," Ven said as Scáth released her grip. Much to her amazement, she saw a tunnel had been carved through the middle of the bridge. "I am going to assume you're comfortable in the darkness, milady?" Ven asked quietly.

"You'd be assuming right," She responded.

"Good," He said. "Wait here, I will be but a moment." As Ven began to crawl towards the Hall he felt Scáth grab him.

"Promise me, you'll return," Ven could barely make out her face in the darkness and his low-light vision was adequate. It was as if she was becoming one with the shadow. What he did see was those large stormy grey eyes staring into him.

"I promise." He felt her hand slip away and he was off.

In the Throne Room was a fight befitting of the ages. The Kintar had fought their way through the entrance, leaving many dead Royal Guards strewn in their wake. None of this would have been achievable if it were not for the Giant-Raptor with bat-like wings leading the assault. These hybrid beasts had beaks capable of piercing the strongest armour, and talons that could cut a man clean in two. The Kintar would crossbreed monstrosities and train them to fit into their ranks, resulting in the creation of many unique beasts. A trainer could often be found saddled securely on its back.

The queen and Rexous were all that was left as the Giant-Raptor cleared the Royal Guards with ease. Rexous stood proudly in front of his Mother, with an axe in one hand and shield in the other. The queen began the incantations of a powerful spell when the three remaining Kintar rushed them. Rexous crouched low as his first enemy approached. Before the Raider had a chance to swing, Rex leapt up connecting his shield with the Raiders' jaw, sending the him flying back, neck broken. As Rex recovered from his shield bash, the second Kintar ran forward letting out a terrifying battle cry. As the Kintar pounded towards him, Rex spun on one foot around the rushing figure, swinging out behind him as he went. The Kintars rushing roar was replaced with a pained shriek as Rex's axe found the spine of the Raider.

A massive peal of thunder rumbled throughout the Hall as the queen unleashed a streak of pink lightning at the Giant-Raptor. It shot straight towards the beak of the beast before ricocheting in the direction of the Rider, annihilating him. The Raptor let out an ear bursting screech that caused all in the room to cover their ears in pain. Rexous was up a second later than the last Raider, and a second too late. The Kintar sliced a large gash down his inner thigh. Rexous dropped to one knee and the Raider met his face with his knee, sending Rex reeling back onto the corpse of a dead guard. The Kintar approached with malice, as the Kyst's hands searched the ground around him. At the last second, he felt the long shaft of a pike, grabbing it, before flicking it upwards, leaving the Kintar no time to respond.

There was no smoke in here for enough magic had been placed upon the Royal Hall to prevent such disasters. Rexous stumbled to his feet and the Giant-Raptor flapped its wings and reeled up. It's wingspan was enough to touch wall to wall, and the Prince looked on in fright as it lunged forward. Rexous tried leaping out of the way but he was grappled tight by the chicken skinned claws. The queen finished another spell, hurling a gout of fire at the colossal monster. It screeched again, feather's burning and hastily flew out the grand entrance, still gripping the prince as he yelled for his queen, his mother.

"Son!" She screamed as only a Mother could. The Raptor and her Son were gone. In the midst of this, she had failed to notice three more Kintar Barbarians had entered the Throne Room and were being led by an old rival. Uthul the Betrayer, a Kyst Elf born of Silva.

"Mourn for your Son while you can, Trilara. Your time is nigh." His words were so sinister they could make even the bravest's skin crawl. But the Queen could not be so easily intimidated

"How dare you Uthul. You have no right!" Trilara yelled and with the wave of her hand, a great burst of arcane energy washed over all three barbarians, throwing them back over a dozen metres and out of the grand hall entrance. Uthul, unaffected, continued forward.

Ven had reached the end of the tunnel leading to the Throne Room. He quietly slid the secret hatch to the side. He saw a room filled with bodies, and two Elves talking at the throne. He went to make his move when the words from the male Kyst stopped him cold.

"You knew this was coming, my queen." Snarled Uthul. Ven was stunned, if Trilara could have predicted this, why wasn't anyone warned.

"You refused me-" before he finished, the queen interrupted.

"-You betrayed us! And continue to do so. What a poor ruler and even poorer husband you would have made." She said to him with venom in her voice. Uthul snarled with contempt. The two were close now.

"You refused me and I told you I would return to destroy all that you held dear. Like I once so dearly held you."

"It was your fantasy Uthul, nothing more. Everything you have done here was born from delusion." She remarked so evenly that Ven could tell it cut the other Kyst deeply. Before anyone had time to think, Uthul slipped a dagger into the queen's Heart. Trilara gave a gasp of pain but it was Uthul, trembling more than her. She grabbed the back of Uthul's head, pulled him close and whispered in his ear.

Ven leaped an epic distance towards them. Running, he grabbed his trident, the handle elongating into a spear as he went. He hurled it at the Kyst with all his might. Uthul caught it with one hand just centimetres from his head. The queen fell weakly to the ground, dagger remaining, blood pouring and staining her elegant dress. Uthul looked to Ven with anger but Ven didn't hesitate in proceeding with his attack. Uthul's expression changed to curiosity before throwing the trident back at him. Ven dropped to his knees, sliding, hair sweeping the floor as he watched the trident pass over him. He effortlessly got back to his feet only to see the Elf gone. So he rushed to his queen's side.

"My queen, where did he go?!" Ven insisted on finding him. The queen surprised Ven by placing a gentle hand on his face.

"Listen to me Ven Devar. You've sought your place in this world your whole life." She spoke softly, which frightened Ven even more.

"Please my queen, let me help you. We can fix this." She rubbed a tear from his face.

"Shh, listen to me. Keep the girl safe, return her to her people. Do this and allow your destiny to take its place." He held his queen tight and gave her all the comfort he could. She pulled a necklace from around her collar and placed it in his hand.

"The symbol of our people, keep it close to your heart, Mighty Hunter." The last thing she did was close his fingers around the pendant before her soul left this world. Ven looked to the grand entrance and saw nothing but bright flames. He felt like he was surrounded by the underworld's hottest fires. Looking back to his queen, the bravest, fairest, and most respectable Kyst he had ever met, he brushed a lock of hair from her face and placed her respectfully on her throne before gently kissing her forehead.

He looked at the necklace in awe. It was carved from the strongest wood in Silva over sixty-thousand years prior and had been a Kyst Royal Artifact ever since. Circular in shape it was embossed with an impossibly detailed image of Silva with a great Cedar tree at its core. He placed it around his neck with honour and reverence. Ven solemnly walked back to the secret passage. Taking one last look at the Great Throne Room, he hung his head and closed the hatch behind him.

Scáth was beginning to wonder if she should try to go after Ven. It had been longer than she expected. She had to admit she had no idea where to look and the possibility of getting lost in these secret passages was enough to keep the idea at bay. She felt a sense of calm when she was in the shadows, like it was a direct route home somehow. She could also see perfectly fine in the darkness when she wanted to; one of the many traits that came with being a ShadowScorn. How she hated that word, it offered nothing but misery and suffering in her eyes. It gave others a feeling that they could do whatever they wanted to with her people, and suffer no ill consequence. Stuck in this passage alone, surrounded by fire, she vowed to never let another ShadowScorn suffer a similar fate.

Scáths fear grew when her head bumped the ceiling, feeling that it was scolding hot. If she stayed here, hidden beneath the bridge, she would either be burnt alive or, if the bridge collapsed, plummet the thousand or so metres to the ground. It was just then she heard her Kyst protector approaching.

"Ven?" Her question echoed through the passage. He didn't respond but her worries vanished when she saw him come around the corner. A smile came across her face but it quickly faded as she noticed tears streaking his cheeks. He approached her silently.

"Milady. Are you okay?" He asked her softly.

"Thanks to you, yes. What happened?" Her eyes scanned him over. He looked to her with defeat.

"I failed to save my queen. By nightfall, Silva will be but a memory." She went to grab his hand but he was already opening the exit. The passage filled with smoke and Ven recoiled from the heat.

"What do we do now?" Scáth managed to ask between coughs.

Ven stuck his head out in an attempt to find something not on fire, something he could descend on. He thought he spotted a tree roughly five metres away directly in front of them.

"We'll have to jump. I'll go first. When I've made it, you'll need to jump on my back, okay?"

Scáth looked out fearfully.

"There is no way I can make it, Ven."

"You'll have to," he responded. "I promise I'll catch you, it's the only way I can get us down." Scáth continued to shake her head in denial. "I believe in you, Scáth. You've survived far worse." Ven gave her a wink that filled her with courage but the doubt lingered heavily in her mind. Scáth began to say something but before she could, Ven leaped with all his might. He flew through the air, emerging through a cloud of smoke and gripped hard onto the tree. He descended a bit knowing Scáth would not maintain height as he did.

"I'm right here, Scáth!" Ven yelled for the girl he so desperately desired to keep safe; an innate feeling he had when he first laid eyes on her, now reinforced by the dying breath of his queen. Scáth remained in the passage for a moment, calming herself. She placed a hand on the wood and flinched in pain for it was on fire now. She backed up slightly and sprang with every ounce of strength. She could see nothing through the smoke but heard Ven. She emerged from the cloud that swirled around her, hand extended. Ven saw her immediately.

"She's too low." He said under his breath. His fingers and feet scraped the tree as he slid down, one hand extended. Their hands met and they grasped each other tightly. Scáth let out a scream and Ven responded with a yelp of pain, as he struggled to pull her up. The strong and refined muscles in his fingers and toes, grasping at the tree, screamed, as the rigid bark tore skin from bone, leaving Ven bleeding harshly.

Scáth raised her free hand and began to climb up Ven's body. Soon her arms were wrapped around him once more. Ven breathed heavily, not used to climbing with the weight of two beings and all the while his lungs were being assaulted by the smoke. Scáth hadn't held anything this tightly since she was a child clinging to her Father.

"See, what did I say?" Ven managed to joke through the pain. She closed her eyes as he began their descent.

CHAPTER FOUR

A Journey's End...

I've thought about how I would leave Silva for years. Ever since I could remember, I've fantasized about finding my real home, my real family. I heard enough times that 'home is where the family is' but Vakar is the only Kyst I could consider kin. Now Silva is gone, not a single survivor has their home. Was it my fault? Did I somehow inadvertently bring Scáth here knowing this would happen? I fear the answer and believe only time will tell. My path is no less obscured but at least I know where my destination lies. It wasn't until we swam the short distance to a sister town of Kyst elves that the loss actually hit me. There were barely two-hundred of the once five-thousand strong and proud Kyst of Silva. My heart eased when I spotted Vakar but it soon felt a heavyweight again when I learned dear Qiri had perished in a necessary sacrifice. An ending that any noble hunter would be proud of, but an untimely ending robs those left grieving of so much more.

-Ven Devar

Ven had spotted the last of Silva's refugees completing their swim to a large Island just off the coast after their onerous exit from Silva. It was known as Sanctuary Island for its dense population of none predatory animals and near unscalable Sea-Cliffs. The fires from Silva were visible from hundreds of kilometres in every direction so it was fortunate that the residents of Sanctuary Island were at the ready. It's population consisted of two symbiotic settlements. Gnomes and Kyst inhabited the island which made it an excellent choice for at least a temporary refuge. Ven and Scáth were the last to arrive in the Village of Hearth where they were met with warm blankets and hot food. Hearth was much different than Silva. Here, they had no need to live above the threats as they were the only predators on the island. However, they were still Kyst and valued many of the same traditions that Silva did. Their homes were built from mighty logs found adrift or washed up on the beach. The island spanned nearly two hundred kilometres long and eighty kilometres wide, and had a population of just over two thousand. Scáth was relieved once again to see that she was not the center of any stares. Much to Ven's disappointment, his reputation extended even here.

It wasn't long before Vakar had found the duo sitting dangerously close to a roaring bonfire. Scáth did not notice the approaching Elf but if she had she would have seen Vakar giving her a dark glare. Ven spotted his companion approaching with haste and a fiery stare.

"Milady, rest here, while I get a better understanding of our current situation." He gave Scáth a smile that warmed her better than the fire, so she contentedly slurped back her soup. A still soggy Ven stood up and strode towards Vakar, meeting him halfway. Without saying anything, they walked a short distance from the Village of Hearth. Vakar didn't make it five minutes before collapsing in tears. Ven fell with him, holding his dearest friend with every ounce of love he had. Ven dare not shed a tear, not now, for he knew he had to be strong. Vakar sobbed for nearly an hour before looking up to his adopted brother.

"It's all those savage's fault, the mindless murdering beasts!" Before Vakar knew it, he was screaming for revenge one moment then sobbing in despair the next. "Now he's gone."

"Qiri is gone for now, yes, but one day you will be reunited. I understand that offers little relief now but you must remember no one is ever truly gone." Ven knew that their beliefs and traditions were all Vakar had to ease his pain.

"What kind of cruelty is this, brother? To meet 'the one' so early and be forced to live the rest of my long and pathetic life without him." Vakar looked at Ven with swollen red eyes, pleading for an answer. Ven hung his head in self-disappointment, unable to comfort him.

"I failed you. I failed Silva and our queen. I was there before she died, and I couldn't stop it." Ven pulled the Royal Artifact out from under his armour. "She died in my arms. Her final words were to return Scáth home and restore our people, Vakar."

Vakar wiped away his tears so he could inspect the necklace. He had never seen it up close and was mesmerized by its intricacy.

"What does this mean then? You're just the King now?" Vakar asked seriously. Ven responded with a slight chuckle.

"No, that isn't my path." He hadn't had a chance to think about what the meaning of the necklace was. Did the queen mean for him to lead their people? How was he supposed to do that and escort Scáth home? Vakar looked at Ven and thought he was doing it again, running away from his responsibilities.

"She gave you the artifact, Ven. Now whether you like it or not, it comes with the duty of leading our people to prosper once more." Vakar stared his dearest friend down.

"Scáth can't wait to return home until I've finished rebuilding our Kingdom can she?" Ven asked rhetorically. Vakar was quick to retaliate.

"So you choose some foreigner you just met over your people?"

Ven remained silent. He knew saying anything further would only lead to greater tempered emotions, so he waited before Vakar filled the silence and changed the subject.

"The leader of these people would like to meet with us. Perhaps they can offer some insight into our troubles." He offered it with little optimism. Ven lifted the necklace and shoved it towards Vakar.

"Here, take it." Vakar looked at it for a long moment before shoving it back to Ven.

"No." He said. "I'm not undoing the last thing she did. Trilara wanted you to have it, whether any of us like it or not." Ven thought his companion sounded bitter. Before he had a chance to say anything, Vakar was up and walking away.

"Find us when you are ready." The hunter heard from a distance. He remained sitting in that patch of lush forest for a long while. For the first time in a very long time, Ven felt scared, but worst of all was the agonizing feeling of helplessness. A conflict between helping Scáth on her journey home and restoring his people's way of life was nipping at his every thought. His queen had quested him with both but which one came first was something Ven was unsure of. Where was Rexous? That upstanding Kyst and all his ego were constantly around when Ven wanted it least. Now he actually needed Rexous, the rightful heir to rule their people and he was nowhere to be found.

"Aha!" Exclaimed the Kyst, as he settled on an idea. He would return to Silva and search for Rexous. Either Ven would find his body and if not, it seemed likely that Rex would also return to Silva. He took a deep breath as he readied himself to begin the first step in his plan. He returned to Scáth who was still seated comfortably by the fire. Ven felt his heart warm as he spotted Scáth sitting with two Kyst children. He paused for a moment to watch the two kids giggling and playing with Scáth's hair.

When Ven walked over to them to join, the two Kyst children immediately stopped playing. They bowed respectfully to the hunter before running off. He let out an auditory sigh as he sat beside Scáth who was wearing a cheeky grin. Ven kept looking into the fire, too worn to acknowledge Scáth's smirk. After a moment of heavy silence, she broke it with the obvious question.

"How did that go?" He looked at her, shrugging doubtfully.

"Nothing is the same, that's all I know." The deep resignation in his voice was clear. She nodded and looked back into the fire. "I have to go back to Silva and look for Rexous, or any survivors for that matter."

Scáth returned a curious gaze. "Alone?"

"Yes." He replied. "The rain will have subdued the fire enough. It needs to be quick and silent so going alone is my best option."

"I understand. Thank you for everything." Her eyes struck Ven in a way that made everything she said seem sweeter.

"I'll be back by sunrise." As he went to leave, he felt her hand grab him again.

"Promise." She insisted.

"I promise."

Ven walked down the island to a peninsula that was the closest point to the mainland. He did this so as not to take a direct path and hopefully avoid any parties left behind searching for stragglers. He also didn't care much to tell anyone other than Scáth where he was going. Halfway through the swim to the mainland, the waves began cresting two-metres and Ven heard a familiar caw from a particular SeaRaven. He rolled his eyes and took a deep gulp of air before submerging. Once Ven had escaped the rough seas above he made it to the shoreline in little time.

He moved through the forest with elegant speed but keen awareness. He stopped and tucked tightly against a tree when he heard the single melodic howl of a wolf. Their songs travelled far but he knew this to be close. Ven's long elven ear flinched when he heard deep breathing from behind him. Turning slowly he saw that remarkable black and white, blue-eyed alpha wolf, sitting patiently just an arm's length away. Ven was amazed more than anything by the wolf's ability to sneak up on him. He hadn't met many creatures who could do that, especially of this size.

The wolf sat there, eventually letting out a great yawn before licking his snout. Ven approached, and put one hand on its thick fury neck. The wolf dragged his massive tongue up the Kyst's arm.

"Aren't you a soft soul in a dangerous and magnificent form." Ven spoke softly to the wolf who slowly squinted his eyes tight. Ven felt that unexplainable connection with the animal. A connection that allowed him to feel their emotions, like so many animals do with humanoids. He felt a sense of protection emanating from this wolf, and Ven felt that similar urge. Soon, the wolf pushed under and against his arm as if in an attempt to lead. He gladly followed his newfound companion. From time to time the alpha would stop and perk his ears up as another singular howl was heard echoing through the valley. Ven assumed the wolves to be protecting the territory from the Kintar, howling occasionally to check in with one another. After a few moments, the alpha brought Ven to four barely recognizable Kintar, mauled and torn to literal shreds. The wolf lowered its head, snarled at the bodies, and looked back to the Kyst.

"Well done." He rubbed the wolf between the ears and thought to give him a handful of seasoned meat from a leather pouch on his belt. Ven looked at the bodies. "Gross. But well done in any case." The wolf graciously took the snack from Ven's hand and they continued in the direction of Silva.

The smoke hung heavy in the air but the flames had mostly died out. Much of the forest was left charred and smouldering. It stung Ven profoundly to see this much nature in ruin. He knew the forest would heal and flourish once again but this much loss of life was palpable. He knew they had made it when he noticed that the giant bridges that had once formed Silva's walkways, had been destroyed and had fallen to the ground. It was late evening now but he could see some stars through the smoke from the forest floor, which was a first. Everything within a kilometre of Silva had felt fire and destruction. The two predators walked through the ash until they reached one completely untouched tree. Nearly a thousand metres up he saw the entrance to the Great Hall. Ven looked towards the beautiful beast, whose eye-level met his own.

"You wanna see?" The wolf walked closer to the tree. "I'll take that as a yes." Ven walked up to the massive trunk, pressing one hand tightly against it. He spoke a Kystin incantation, revealing a door that receded into the tree. Inside was a wide spiral staircase, carved from the base that curled and stretched all the way to the top.

Ven went in and the wolf followed quickly behind. It was a long walk but the agile beast passed and ran ahead, up the stairs. Ven was astonished by the sheer size of the wolf and how that fact did nothing to diminish his dexterity. When Ven reached the top, he popped out behind the throne and noticed the alpha was already out in the hall. The hunter's heart skipped a beat knowing that someone had already opened this secret passage. Ven immediately drew his short-sword, and the wolf, seeing this fell to attention. He scanned the room for any activity but all was still. It was an epic bloodbath of Kyst and Kintar crowding the floor's surface. Ven edged through the pools of congealed blood towards the throne. An intertwined mass of vines and plants, the throne was an ever-changing presence in the hall. As he came around to the front he witnessed the pinnacle of his failure. Rexous' body was half leaning on the throne with one hand tightly grasping his mothers, the queen's. The other arm hung to the side with a small but steady trickle of blood running onto the floor. Rexous' clothes were torn to shreds and he had deep claw gashes raked across his body. Ven approached slowly and knelt beside them. He reached out to check for a pulse, for any sign of life from the Prince.

Before he knew it, Rexous' eyes snapped open and he gripped tightly onto Ven's arm, sliding a dagger into Ven's lower stomach. He let out a violent gulp for air as the shock stole his breath. The wolf snarled and bared its teeth grievously but did not intervene. Rexous looked deeply into the eyes of his rival. The hatred Ven saw cut deeper than any dagger had. At the center of all that pained emotion was him, Ven Devar. With his free hand, Ven grabbed Rexous' arm that held the dagger, and pushed him away, removing the blade in the process. Ven tumbled backwards, clutching at the wound which was bleeding profusely.

The wolf moved closer to Rex, biting at the air around him. "No." Ven uttered, which was enough to stay the alpha.

"You did this." Was all that the weak Rexous could mumble before slumping back against the throne, unconscious. Ven was left holding his abdomen, catching his breath for many minutes before he went to fill his wound with a Kyst salve. He winced briefly as he tightly wrapped a cloth around his waist to help stem the bleeding and pack the medicine. It was far from his first combat wound and would be far from the last. The alpha continued around the room, sniffing intently. Ven's attention was split between his own pain and immediately going to dress the wounds that Rexous had suffered during his harrowing battle with Giant-Raptor. He made sure to pack Rexous' wounds tightly. They had a long trek ahead of them, before any real help could be called.

As Ven heaved Rex over his shoulders, he heard the alpha muster a growl from the back of its throat, and the distant sound of whooshing air. As the wind stirred, the wolf and hunter paused, looking to the grand entrance that now, remained open, without any doors. With a deafening screech, the Giant-Raptor swooped inside, snapping ferociously. The wolf leapt at the monster but was thrown back against the wall by it's mighty leathery wings. Ven caught this out of the corner of his eye while lowering Rex to the ground. Dropping the prince harder than he wanted, Ven covered his ears as the Raptor let out an ear-bursting screech. Ven drew his trident as the Raptor soared towards him. Lining up his pole-arm in hand, with the monstrosity that quickly approached, he threw the trident with uncanny expertise. It found its mark and sank directly into the bird's breast but did little to slow it down. Before Ven had a chance to react the Giant Beasts wing rammed him in the chest, hurling him against the throne and into a crumpled pile on the floor. The Raptor continued through and up, hovering in the high ceilings. After his dramatic landing face-first with the floor, Ven barely had time to roll out of the way as the

Raptor dived towards him, bearing those razor-sharp talons that had slashed so many Kyst to pieces. Ven stopped rolling just in time to avoid another stomp from the talons. As he rolled back the other way, he unsheathed his short-sword, held it out and let the Raptor sever its own foot off with the momentum. It shrieked in pain as the colossal wings reeled its body back. Ven threw his legs up and behind him, rolling to his feet in a low defensive stance.

As the Raptors foot skidded across the floor, the alpha wolf jumped onto the throne and leapt into the air, biting down hard onto the beak of the bird. Ven had seen this tactic used by wolves before, embedding their fangs into the snout or muzzle of animals, literally choking them to death. The wolf locked its jaw and the Raptor tumbled onto its back from the sheer weight. The two beasts flailed about in a struggle of life and death. Ven was quick to rush up to the brawling animals and plummet his sword into the heart of the Raptor.

The wolf let go of the beak once the Raptor had stopped twitching, and let out a long howl of victory. Ven was thankful for having such a deadly hunting companion for this particular foe. The Kyst studied all life around them and knew that wolves were the best pack hunters in the entirety of Litore. A pack was a perfectly well-oiled machine that took every precaution and studied every aspect possible in regards to their prey, and then simultaneously went to work with perfect communication, leading to flawless execution. The Kyst Hunters were inspired and learned much from the wolves that they shared the coast with. Ven Looked to the alpha, and the wolf returned his gaze.

"I guess it was coming back for food." The wolf gave a quick exhale of the nose and padded over to Ven, sniffing around his stab wound. Ven rubbed him between the ears but the wolf continued over to nuzzle the underside of Rex before looking back to Ven with its large, brilliant coastal-blue eyes. He was grateful at the wolf's indication to carry Rexous and went to placing the Prince on the alpha's large back. His legs and hands barely brushed the earth as he lay belly forward on the canine. Ven was quick to usher the wolf out of the Throne Room. He took no extra time for a final look around, he just wanted to be gone.

Soon, the duo were sauntering through the forest under the darkness of night. Ven moved slowly as the pain from his wound was beginning to worsen. The hunter paused for a moment to lean up against a tree for a quick rest. The alpha let out a long and full howl that echoed even further than usual through the smouldering forest. Ven watched the wolf closely who had his ears perked and head high expecting a response from his pack. When no reply came he lowered his head, clearly sniffing out any threats.

As far as Ven could tell they were alone but the wolf was soon pushing his head against the Kysts' lower back, attempting to get him on the move again. So, with a pained sigh, Ven began to head towards the beach. He couldn't help but notice that the alpha was staying closer than usual so Ven broke out into a light run. Running side by side, the wolf suddenly dodged to the left creating a gap between them. As he looked across to the alpha, Ven saw an arrow filling that gap, striking the ground. Running even quicker now, Ven heard another arrow whistling his way. He ducked low into a roll as a rusty and blood-stained Kintar arrow flew over him. He stumbled to get back to his feet as his wound diminished his focus and was bleeding much worse. The wolf was right there to help him get going again. Now, the pair were in a full sprint avoiding a rainfall of arrows. The nasty sound of a Kintar battle cry filled Ven with an uncontrollable rage. The wolf responded in a series of short higher pitched howls in an effort to call his pack to his side. It became evident to Ven that the arrows had been herding them into an ambush when a Kintar Barbarian jumped in front of him. Ven didn't slow as the Barbarian lifted his Ax. The hunter, drawing a dagger, ducked under the Kintar's arm and dragged the blade down his brachial artery. Ven kept running, confident that the Barbarian would not pursue. Before long, running was all the wolf and hunter could do to avoid the barrage of swinging Kintar and hailing arrows.

Ven knew that all their momentum was lost when he spotted a four-metre tall Ogre came barreling through the trees. It kicked the alpha, sending the yelping beast half a dozen metres through the air. Rexous soared like a ragdoll, connecting hard against a tree. Ven drew his bow and knocked an arrow aimed for the Ogre's ear, as soon as he let it loose the Ogre turned towards Ven causing the arrow to break against its callous ridden forehead. Ven wasn't sure where his companion ended up but spotted Rexous contorted against a dead cedar. He unhooked his trident and sprinted over to protect the Prince. The trident was magnificent in design. The end was weighted and had three blades stretching up and into a singular razor-sharp point. All Ven could do to keep the Ogre at a distance was to sporadically poke at the beast's flesh every time it got too close. He knew his time was limited as the Kintar archers would soon draw swords and surround them. Ven spotted the alpha stalking quietly behind the Ogre before leaping and tearing off a chunk of its ankle. The Ogre howled and a hatchet flew into the tree next to Vens head. As he looked to the hatchet and back towards the forest, a wave of raiders came streaming from out of the trees. He cut, sliced, and stabbed quicker than he thought possible. A bloodied stack of dead and dying Kintar was beginning to form at his feet. For a split second, Ven looked to Rexous who was still unconscious at the base of the tree. He turned back to the hoard of Kintar swarming him and when a club met his eyes, Ven hit the ground before he knew what happened. When the beating began he curled himself up hoping his armour would take most of the blunt trauma. Through the excruciating pain, he thought it odd these Kintar weren't trying to kill him, but instead mercilessly beat him into unconsciousness.

The alpha bared its blood dripping fangs at the Ogre, snarling with the threat of death. The Ogre had never seen a wolf this large before but he had squashed a hundred of the pesky dogs and thought that this one would meet a similar fate. The Ogre kicked at the alpha who bit off a few toes as the foot retracted. The Ogre fell forward on his marred foot and ankle, swiping his 45 kilogram arm against the body of the wolf. This time, the alpha collided headfirst into the side of a great cedar and lay still, whimpering quietly at the base. Soon the sounds of a pack attacking could be heard. Vicious, guttural noises sounded and one by one Ven felt the kicks lessen, and the punches subside. He lifted his head from under his arms to see a fierce battle between wolves, Kintar, and one stubborn Ogre. It was not a battle easily fought. The wolves were outnumbered but they used their speed and agility to their advantage. Three to four wolves would run through the clearing, biting a single target, while another three to four wolves lined up for their next run. Despite making the most out of their numbers, they were suffering at great cost to their own with each strike. Ven dragged himself over to Rexous, laying on top of him in some attempt to protect the rightful ruler of Silva.

A group of six wolves including the now recovered alpha encircled the Ogre, snapping at the beast and each biting down on flesh at just the opportune time. Occasionally, the ugly monster would connect with a solid punch, sending a aolf flying through the air. Before long, the pack had bitten the legs of the Ogre so bad he was slipping in his own puddle of blood. Eventually, the alpha knocked him over and the pack piled onto his body, shredding the now fallen giant.

Ven felt a pinch of excruciation as he took an arrow to the thigh from a new hoard of arriving Kintar. Letting out a scream of pain, he held tighter to Rexous. A Kintar that spotted Ven wounded, and had just lodged his spear into the belly of a wolf, ran over to the hunter, striking him in the head with a club.

After the alpha saw the damage done to the pack he let out a long howl, calling for retreat. Most of the pack lay with swords or spears protruding from them, but never without a disembowelled Kintar beside. The rest of the wolves were severely injured and would likely succumb to their wounds, perhaps save a few. The alpha was last to leave but spotted Ven laying face down in a pile of bodies. He leaped and sprinted towards the hunter, effortlessly smashing into a handful of Kintar as he went. Skidding to a stop, the wolf clasped it's jaws onto the thick leather armour surrounding Ven and sprinted off to safety.

The Kyst woke only for a few seconds at a time while being carried through the forest, held tightly in the alpha's mouth. The sensation and confusion of it all was what quickly drew the Kyst back into a blackout. He was suddenly awoken by several long licks across his face and the alpha using his snout to flop Ven's head around on the pebbled beach. Ven lifted his arm to stop the wolf. Slightly rolling over, he got to one elbow and immediately passed out from the grievous pain. By now most of Ven's body was black and blue, including one eye swollen shut from the strike that originally knocked him low. Before Ven lost total consciousness, he passed out to the distant sight of Sanctuary Island.

The majestic, strong, and intelligent wolf looked to the Island that Ven had weakly signalled towards and considered if he could swim it or not. He looked down at the Elf laying on the beach and lowered his head. The wolf was clearly considering what to do. He slowly turned to view the forest and let out a long, melancholic howl. The wolf fought to keep his eyes open and waited patiently, hoping for any response from his pack, hoping he still had a pack to even lead. The alpha slowly looked back to the Kyst once more. The wolf sensed days prior that the girl in the woods was a threat to the forest but when the alpha saw Ven reaching out, he had ignored his intuition. No wolf had felt the unique presence of a humanoid as this one. It was much like how the wolves communicated with each other, with actions and emotion replacing words. But, it was the fact that this alpha could sense everything about this Kyst that had convinced him that Ven was at no fault for the destruction of the forest or his pack.

The wolf nuzzled Vens head again and laid down beside him. Ven didn't awake at first but after the wolf gave a series of loud snorts and whines, Ven rolled onto the beast's massive back. The wolf padded over to the water and soon his thick fur was soaked as he began swimming over to Sanctuary Island under the dawn's earliest light. Ven was awake for most of this part of the journey. It wasn't the cold splashing water that woke him, rather a particular squawking SeaRaven overhead.

CHAPTER FIVE
... is a Journey's Beginning

For five agonizing days, I lay in bed going over everything that transpired. I had hoped that for a short time after finding Rexous, things would be okay. Those damned Kintar always made little sense to me. Killing was the pinnacle of their culture and religion. They derived everything from entertainment to wealth through the simple act. Since my training began as a hunter of Silva at the age of ten, I found extraordinary gratitude and humbleness from my kills. Every animal I struck low with an arrow was a sentient creature. We only killed in need of food or defence and for that, we Kyst honour each kill as a life passing from this realm to the next. As I lay here beaten, bruised, and wounded, I've never felt so close to this death I have inflicted on so many. Now, Rexous is truly gone. I failed, again. And yet was this not what I wanted? To be free? Available to go where I want, when I want. Exploring every shoreline, mountain peak, desert, and forest on Litore. Surviving that, perhaps travelling to distant lands where new adventure and foe could be found. It is undeniable that Scáth holds a view of my heart and soul and that guiding her home safely is an essential duty. Had My queen not instructed me so, or our instant connection had not been found, I would still find delivering Scáth home safely to be of the utmost importance for none other than what honour demands of a warrior. I must speak with the leaders of these two villages and garner all the variables at play. Scáth has been watching over my recovery, for which I am eternally grateful. Her mere presence was enough to fill my spirit. However, Vakar had been to see me less than expected, explaining to the healers he was too busy with our people. I fear there is still much to lose in the aftermath of Silva's destruction.

* * *

-Ven Devar

Ven was awoken by a compilation of boisterous knocks on the door of his driftwood cabin. He winced getting out of bed as he coddled his abdomen. He was delighted the wound hadn't opened today and thought the stitches might finally hold. He hung a robe around his bandaged body and opened the door to a particularly grumpy gnome.

"Mister Ven Devar?" Ven raised a brow, surprised by the oddly deep voice.

"Yes?" the gnome held out a bundle of clothes bound together by twine.

"Our leaders request you wear these to your meeting." Ven grabbed the bundle of bright green bamboo clothes.

"Uhm, thanks?" Ven muttered awkwardly. The gnome hardly acknowledged him as he left. Ven shut the door and placed the clothes on the table. He admired the architecture of the village; the resourcefulness of reclaiming wood lost at sea or washed up on a beach seemed brilliant. He untied the twine and was amazed by the softness and durability of the raiment. He had seen little crops of bamboo on the island and was told by Scáth that the residents farmed it, turning the bamboo into a number of useful products. The clothes hugged his body nicely and were neatly cuffed with a short but stiff collar. He stepped outside and was met by a soft breeze and some of the last sunshine of autumn. He had some time before the meeting with Lord Tolmie Trickfoote and Queen Ilthanis Veldove so the Kyst decided on a walk to clear his mind.

He took a steep and narrow path down one of the sea cliffs to a beach. Upon reaching the shore, he wiggled his butt into a tall section of accumulated pebbles and found comfort in his solitude. He closed his eyes and began to fall into a meditative state. In the state between meditation, much like the state between sleep and consciousness, Ven was violently jolted awake by the startling squawk of that same SeaRaven. Much to his surprise, the SeaRaven had landed next to him and was perched on a log, staring inquisitively at the hunter.

"What do you actually want?" Ven asked, furrowing his brow. The SeaRaven, with her long webbed feet, hopped about a few times and ruffled her dark purple feathers. It blinked blankly at Ven and cawed once more. Ven drooped his head in defeat and continued to meditate. After several undisturbed minutes, he slightly opened his right eye to see if the bird was still there. In response, the bird who hadn't moved a feather cocked its head in curiosity. He quickly closed his eye and thought perhaps, much like the alpha wolf, that he could attach to this pestering bird. The SeaRaven had started bothering him since the start of the year, their interactions only growing in frequency. Soon he felt anxious but knew it not to be his own anxiety, rather the SeaRaven's. He understood that this animal was trying to protect him as much as the alpha had. Ven opened his eyes and put his arm out for the bird, who happily fluttered up. The two shared a gaze for admittedly longer than Ven had anticipated. He didn't understand why all of a sudden these animals were reaching out to him. He considered that something within him must have changed that broke down a previous barrier. He stood up, and the SeaRaven flapped up into the sky.

"Well, if you insist on following me, at least keep an eye on things." Ven laughed a little when the bird cawed in a well-timed response. He began to walk up the thin and dangerous path along the cliff back toward his meeting. He hadn't seen Scáth all day but thought that may be for the best. Ven desired a clear head when speaking to the leaders of this safe haven. He assumed Vakar would be in attendance, there were no ranking sages remaining from Silva but he was best suited and talented for leading them. So many of the duties that used to be on the masters now fell to him. Ven certainly didn't yearn for royalty and honestly thought that he would make a poor monarch. His heart tugged for adventure and exhilaration. Who could live their entire life sheltered, only indulging in their own culture when there was so much to be experienced? Perhaps the arrival of Scáth was rather a test than the answer to his solitude. If he did stay now and rule the people of Silva, would he not feel a sense of belonging.

Before the hunter knew it, he was walking up the front steps to a beautiful but humble building that was prominently used as a town hall. He pulled on the large shellfish handle and found a warmly lit hall with a great table near the back of the room. There he saw a little gnome sitting on a high chair. He had salt and pepper, clean-cut hair and a beard. His raiment was similar to Ven's but decorated like that of a nobleman. The Kyst elf sitting across from the gnome was a several-hundred-year-old female with iridescent silver hair and a face as beautiful as the Gods they were descendants of. She wore long and flowing silken robes that were covered from train to neck in leaf patterns. To Ven's expectations, he saw his dear friend sitting next to the gnome.

"Ahh, we were thinking of sending a messenger for ya!" Tolmie exclaimed in a jovial mood. Tolmie and Ilthanis stood to greet their guest, but Vakar remained seated. Ven bowed low to each leader before sitting next to Ilthanis. He was caught off guard to hear the gnome speaking Kystin and not the more common tongue of Litore but remembered these two races to be close neighbours on Sanctuary Island. Ilthanis turned her powerful glistening brown eyes to Ven.

"It is an honour to finally sit down with the 'Mighty Ven Devar' of Silva."

Ven tried to hide the disdain he felt at the sound of that title. "Nonsense, the pleasure should be all mine, Your Highness. I'm not but a humble Kyst doing what I was taught." Ven lowered his head in respect. Vakar looked at Ven, not with pride but irritation. Vakar was still on the fence about if what happened to Silva was Ven's fault or not, and here was yet another queen barraging him with compliments.

"Yee Kyst and your propriety." Tolmie laughed. "How about yee earn your keep and show us how mighty yee really are by going on a hunt for the people of Hearth, eh?"

Ilthanis eye's widened. "He's not your errand boy, Tolmie," she said sharply to the excitable gnome. "Besides, he needs to heal." Ven felt awkward about their bickering and looked to Vakar in an instinctual plea for support but felt only coldness in his direction.

"Actually, Your Highness, if it's all the same, I think a hunt would do me well."

Before anyone had a chance to respond, Tolmie Trickfoote jumped up onto the massive cedar table.

"It's settled then! Once we've adjourned, I'll prepare me best gatherers to join yee." Ilthanis looked helpless but decided that, if Ven was happy, then she had little to fret about. Vakar took this as an opportunity to achieve what he thought was important.

"If we're done discussing games, then may we address the real concerns?" His tone left the room quiet. Ven couldn't help but notice the entire comment was delivered with Vakar staring him down, to which Ven returned the gaze

"Aye," Tolmie began. "It be a true shame about the burning of thee spectacular Silva. My deepest apologies, lads. I know first hand it ain't an easy thing." Ven and Vakar both nodded in gratitude, and Ilthanis spoke softly.

"I was dear friends with Trilara, so I assure you, I've felt this loss closely. For that reason, and many more, I offer you any aid I may muster in helping the fine folk of Silva. Though I am curious what you plan to do with the remainder of your people?"

Ven was quick to pull the necklace from under his stiff green clothes and hand it to Ilthanis.

"Perhaps you could speak a little more to this?" Ilthanis was near speechless as Ven handed her the necklace. She held it carefully in her impossibly delicate hands. She was not attempting to learn but rather savour every line and inspect every leaf carved into the pendant.

"They who wear this is the ruler of Silva. Surely you're aware of that, Ven Devar," said the queen.

"I was with her when she passed. Uthul 'The Betrayer' is to blame for her death. She gave me this and quested me with the safety of Scáth and Silva's people."

Tolmie took the opportunity to pipe up in a tone unbefitting of the scenario.

"Then a Mighty King you are! A rabbit's tale to being a hunter, royalty is far more entertaining." Tolmie cleared his throat and settled back down when none out of three Kyst elves showed any appreciation for his commotion.

"As you can see, the only leader we have is not very committed. You won't even call them 'your' people, will you? Always dreaming of other places, never actually here." Vakar spoke with spite. Tolmie's big bushy eyebrows raised an impressive height at the comment.

"Perhaps my lack of interest does not lie with the location but its inhabitants. The sooner you accept I had nothing to do with this, the sooner we can begin rebuilding Silva and our lives," Ven responded and felt his heart rate launch, but he dared not reveal his inner animosity. Vakar was rehearsed with his response.

"Will that be before or after you take your lost girl halfway across Litore?" He set his jaw and stared defiantly at Ven. Ven ground his teeth at the audacity and rather erratic behaviour of his dearest companion. Ilthanis was surprised by the arguing between two who were known to be so close.

"Perhaps, my young Kyst, it is too soon to talk about such things. Time to heal mental and physical wounds should never be rushed. A shame such a terrible thing should befall such a sweet-hearted girl." Vakar rolled his eyes wide, but Ven just looked to the ever-wise Ilthanis.

"Indeed it is." Ven found himself awkwardly clearing his throat. "I am honour-bound to safely return her to her people, Your Highness."

"Where's thee shadow gal from anyhow? Never seen or heard of her kind before," Tolmie spoke with a little more reserve this time. Ven and Vakar truthfully did not know, aside from what little Scáth had told them. Ilthanis looked to her long-time friend and fellow leader seated across the table. She respected Tolmie as much as anyone in his station, but Ilthanis always enjoyed seeing the tiny man in a highchair that wasn't all that different from a chair used for most children.

"They live in a small fortified city to the east near Moon Mountain. Although, from what I have heard whispered, they've done quite well in expanding the city. Nearly a thousand years ago, their settlement was touched by a powerful source of darkness and shadow, leaving its settlers of humans, elves, and dwarves forever altered. The city now goes by ShadowScorn."

"Interesting, Scáth told me her family name is ShadowScorn," added Ven.

"Then she must be of some repute," responded Ilthanis. "Perhaps her people are in true need of her."

"Why was she a couple of months journey from her home then?" asked Tolmie, to which Ilthanis had another answer.

"Religious heretics from the west claim these ShadowScorn were put in front of the world as a test of faith. The followers of the benevolent Goddess Sesara, the deity of life and sustenance. The truth behind the priests who advocate for this behaviour is unknown to me, but it's clear wherever these shadow graced people end up is a truly heinous place."

Ven could feel a rage brewing inside him that he had only felt a few times in his life. The Kyst were religious people, offering prayer to

Āina and Kaia, lover God and Goddess of the land and sea. Yet, Ven never found much verification in religion. Divine creatures rarely ever seemed concerned with the well-being of their followers, only ever-demanding patronage or sacrifice and showing up often enough to be as common as a legend.

"As the only true Kyst monarch here, what would you have me do?" Ven asked Ilthanis with complete vulnerability.

Ilthanis looked to Vakar, who wore a desperate scowl, but she noted a deep sadness on the young and undeniably skillful sage. And when she looked back to Ven, it was easy to tell that he had suffered greatly and lost much of what he considered he knew about himself.

"Go on our hunt, Ven Devar. With your added people, we will need more food than ever. Upon your return, we will hold a meeting to discuss Tolmie and I's decision."

"Thank you for your wise counsel and aid, Queen Ilthanis." Ven nodded low and stood from his seat. Tolmie jumped up and led Ven out of the hall. Before he exited the building, the hunter looked over his shoulder to see Vakar being overly emotional to Ilthanis, and knew his friend to be that way with no one but Qiri and himself. Ven's attention, however, was quickly diverted away from the peculiar sight as Tolmie tugged on his shirt tails.

"So, when do yee wanna leave? I can have me gnomes ready by dawn."

"Dawn sounds nice, Tolmie." Ven gave the 'larger than life' gnome a courteous smile. The pair walked into town, passing a cluster of small shacks that acted as a town market.

"I'm curious, and correct me if I am wrong, but your people were on this island before the Kyst, no?"

Tolmie proudly responded. "Aye, we've been here far longer than any other race."

"Then why did you let the elves join you? Surely it was yours to keep to yourselves, the way you liked it."

Tolmie stopped in the town square, where the tree's parted to reveal a vista of breathtaking proportions. On a clear day, you could see the mainland and nearly a hundred different islands that made up a small fraction of the massive archipelago in the north of Litore. The market was a bustling little downtown of two races co-existing perfectly.

"Hahaha, yee young elves ain't so bad before ya grow up." Ven wasn't sure if he should be insulted or not but listened anyway. "We gnomes are an opportunistic bunch. When something new arrives or something old changes, it shouldn't be feared but embraced to its full potential. Fortunately enough, all that time ago, the leaders of these Kyst thought likewise."

By the time Tolmie was done, Ven had a noticeable smile on his face.

"In that case, could you point me to where Scáth has been staying?" Tolmie smirked, although Ven didn't notice due to the height difference.

"Aye, yee're getting it." Tolmie nudged the side of Ven's knee and pointed to a bungalow that had been Scáth's residence since her arrival.

"Thank you, Tolmie. It's been a pleasure speaking with you today." Ven nodded appreciatively before walking in the direction of Scáth's home. Ven was still walking with a bit of a limp, although he knew stretching would aid the healing process. He paused to collect a small bundle of flowers that would open up and glow a soft purple at night. He hesitated outside her door for a few moments. With the fourth attempt at knocking on Scáth's door failing, it swung open to show the ShadowScorn standing there with a sarcastically disappointed look.

"Afternoon, milady," Ven said, offering the flowers. Scáth's eyes turned a visibly brighter white.

"Why, thank you, Ven Devar." She grabbed the flowers and left the door. She filled a glass with water and put her flowers by the window. Ven walked only a few paces inside.

"How are you healing?" she asked, and Ven detected genuine concern behind her question.

"Better every day. I believe now that I am up and back in nature, I will heal all the sooner."

Scáth smiled. "You are a curious one." Ven was bashful at the comment but remembered why he had come here in the first place.

"I have a proposition." Ven was worried he had said something wrong as Scáth lost her jovial smile. "Somehow, one way or another, you're going to be reunited with your homeland. If you really want that to happen, I invite you to join me on a hunt so that you may learn or re-learn the ways to survive in the wild."

"Oh. I don't know, Ven." Scáth seemed overly reserved, and Ven didn't hold out much hope for a positive answer but thought her eyes changed to a darker shade. He noticed the scimitar that he had given her during the downfall of Silva and walked over to it.

"There is nothing to fear on this island, Scáth. It would be the essentials to get you home." Ven paused and grasped the sword. "Back to your family." Scáth looked at him accusingly.

"I'm not a warrior, or a killer, got it?" The ShadowScorn was harsh with her words.

"No, but you'll have to be," Ven said sorrowfully while handing her the sword. Scáth took it reluctantly, and Ven wasted no time in exiting her cabin. She stood there, feeling silly for pushing her only friend here away. Then she felt far worse when she thought of him as a true friend unlike ever before, especially in ShadowScorn. Ven had no appetite this day and went back to his cabin to rest.

Vakar and Ilthanis had supper together that night in the queen's private bungalow overlooking the ocean. It was the third night the pair had secreted themselves away for debates on tradition and sharing detailed histories of one another's home.

"I must admit, Vakar, it has been most thrilling and entertaining having you here to discuss such universal topics. Yet you must know, I am privy to the fact that you have ulterior motives." As the queen placed her napkin on her empty plate, it rose and floated away inside.

"Your Highness, 'ulterior motives' is a rather malevolent description. It is true I have been focused on my people and thought of little else since our arrival. I desire what is only best for them."

"And what would that be in your words?"

"I would suggest, if I may, having Ven make you temporary ruler of our people. This will help achieve the safe arrival of Scáth to her people and Ven completing our queen's last wishes while simultaneously allowing us to rebuild Silva." Vakar seemed completely genuine to Ilthanis, and yet she was surprised she did not think of the plan herself. Vakar could tell he had surprised and possibly pleased the queen with his idea.

"What role would you play in all this?" she inquired.

"The other sages and I are well practised in our people's architecture, we will lead the team that restores our once great city," Vakar said while pouring the duo more wine.

"I'm impressed, Vakar. You truly are what everyone makes you out to be." The queen finished her wine and stood from her seat, brushing her hand along Vakar's shoulder as she passed.

"Goodnight, 'Vakar the Cunning'." The young Kyst remained on the patio for a while, looking over the moonlit ocean.

It was still dark outside when Ven met Tolmie and a handful of his gatherers a short distance outside of Hearth. Ven was pleased to see a few hunters from Silva were also there awaiting the ritual beginning of the hunt. Torches were set up in a wide ring, and Ilthanis stood in the centre of it all wearing ceremonial garb. Ven was undeniably disappointed when he didn't spot Scáth but proceeded closer, determined to have a meditative hunt.

"Well, if it isn't thee guest of honour!" yelled Tolmie triumphantly. Ven bowed low to the nobleman and his gnome comrades.

"I look forward to sharing our knowledge and traditions with one another over the next few days," Ven said politely.

"Don't be mad if we outperform ya, elf!" One of the gnomes nudged his friend as they began to laugh among each other. Ven noticed this gnome was dirtier than the rest, a healthy coating of earth. He even had a chipmunk that seemed to perpetually hang out all over his body.

"Well, let us see if your little legs can keep up." Ven gave a cheeky wink. At first, he had thought the joke didn't land until all six gnomes, including Tolmie, burst into uncontrollable laughter. Ven looked to the three other Kyst elves.

"This should be fun," said a hunter who clearly wasn't the most excited about spending so much time with the unpredictable and light-hearted race. Soon the assembled party fell silent at the heed of Ilthanis. Behind her were several Kyst from Hearth playing a series of wood-carved flutes in a slow thought-provoking tone. Each Kyst took turns being blessed by Ilthanis as she spoke a prayer.

"I ask that Āina, Father of our forests, bless this hunter with your skill and abundance. I ask that Kaia, Mother to our oceans, bestow upon this hunter your compassion and deadliness." At the end of each prayer, Ilthanis would then plant a kiss on the forehead of the hunter and individually mark their face with dyed sap.

Ven wasn't sure if it was a coincidence that at the end of his prayer,

Scáth was now standing by the gnomes, evidently dressed for the wild. He shot her a smile from across the circle of torches, to which she responded in kind.

Soon the worst part of the hunt, in Ven's mind, was over, and he was able to do what he loved most. The party consisted of six gnomes, Four Kyst, and Scáth. Not the most traditional hunting party, but one Ven was excited to journey with. It would also be a novel experience not having to contend with the average predators like on the mainland. Plus, it would offer a great training ground for Scáth.

The party had walked half a day's journey east, along the island's southern coast. In that time Ven had got to know the gnomes a little better, especially the one who was a friend to most forest critters. By now, several hare, songbirds, and squirrels had begun to follow the filthy gnome. One of the hunters had looked to Ven as if asking permission to hunt the critters that were emerging to follow the gnome. Ven, eyes wide, shook his head discreetly.

"Alright, how do you do that?" Ven questioned curiously. The barely 90-centimetre tall gnome chuckled.

"Perhaps if you watch long enough, the answer will reveal itself to you. Although I fear given your nature as a hunter, the animals of the world may have a hard time connecting with you." Ven considered that was a fair assumption but knew otherwise.

"What is your name, my friend?" Ven hadn't spent too much time around gnomes but found this one to be of great company.

"Athvar 'The Undusted'." The little gnome gave a great laugh at the sound of his own funny name. Ven wore a wide smile at the ability all gnomes had to find humour and optimism in almost anything. As Athvar and Ven walked together, he noticed Scáth was being shown by the other gnomes and elves all the edible and poisonous plants they passed.

When the party settled in to make camp, the two races shared several methods that could make life easier. The Kyst hunters were most impressed by the gnomes teaching them how to make effective blankets from moss and flora in only a few moments. Ven sat around the fire with the rest of the party, seated between Scáth and Athvar. He sat there with his hood up and his knees to his chest, fitting himself warmly under his heavy PumaSheep cloak. Eventually, one of the gnome gatherers, who Ven thought was undeniably sweet on Scáth, asked her to regale us with a tale from her homeland. She wasn't convinced at first, but as it turned out, everyone around the campfire was eager to listen. Although she had not admitted it to him, it was beginning to make sense to Ven that Scáth was of no-insignificant importance.

"Near a thousand years ago, a small mining population had settled in an abandoned town. Most of the new residents were a poor sort who had moved there in the hopes of mining resources that were long ago thought to be depleted. One dark and dreary autumn eve such as this, the settlers were all haunted by a ghostly figure. My great grandfather experienced what most did that night. Everyone in town endured their own death, left to then roam the world aimlessly without purpose, neither dead nor alive. Until, after what felt like an eternity, everyone awoke in their beds the following morning. Forever scarred by shadow." Scáth could tell that the entire camp was tense and she noticed the gnome who requested the story was nearly under his blanket in fright.

"Well, not a one here can top that story, I bet yee!" Laughed Tolmie, cutting the tension. Even Ven was wide-eyed at the tale and was relieved to see his fellow Kyst were as well. Soon the gnome pulled the blanket down from over his head, uttering.

"Thanks for sharing that story, Lady Scáth," he said before immediately going to sleep, well hidden from anything that could get him. Even though Tolmie assured Ven that no one would need to take watch due to the lack of predators. Ven found himself uncomfortable with the idea and stayed up long past everyone else.

The hunter, weary from his wounds, eventually closed his eyes, falling into the meditative state that was the equivalent to how elves in Litore slept. He found himself stuck in what he thought was a dream, as a baby lost at sea in a dinghy. In this dream, Ven was forced to lay with his back against the hull, slowly shifting with the waves. Rain begins to pound against his face, and the swells begin to rise, violently rocking the boat. The constant discomforting screech of a SeaRaven can be heard and seen flying above in wide circles against the blinding clouds. A true sense of dread and loneliness fills Ven as he defencelessly lays there adrift at sea. The dream ended as it always did, with the hollow thud of boats bumping and a single Kyst fisherman jumping aboard.

Ven jolted forward from his slumber with a heavy sweat on his brow. It was his oldest nightmare and, to this day, woke him up with a powerful fright. He would convince himself that he would not be afraid when he found himself in that dream. Alas, each time it occurred, it was as if he was experiencing it for the first time.

"Nightmare?" came a soft and sweet voice from Scáth, who had rolled over to face Ven. The hunter nodded, embarrassed.

"I often have nightmares now… about the night I was taken," Scáth said sadly. Ven instinctually grabbed her hand and held it tight. Scáth smiled and closed her eyes again, happy to be in the company of someone as chivalrous as Ven Devar.

When Scáth opened her eyes again, the sun was rising far behind the thick clouds, and by now, most of the camp was waking up. Shortly after noticing Ven was missing, she spotted him walking through the woods toward camp with several small game in hand. He dropped them off to his fellow Kyst.

"Would you demonstrate how we prepare and cook our game?" One of the Kyst hunters graciously took the animals. Ven stood aside as the gnomes gathered around the Kyst, who was skinning a rabbit and giving prayer to its sacrifice. The Kyst always gave thanks to the animals that died in the effort to fuel their own mind and souls. The gnomes thought it to be rather silly since the animals were already dead, but Scáth found admiration in it. Ven soon noticed Athvar collecting his things for the day away from the now prepared food. He made a small plate on a leaf and brought it to his new friend.

"Breakfast?" Ven offered the food. Athvar continued about his business rather distantly.

"It's not as tasty once yar got to know them," Athvar replied rather coldly but Ven took no offence.

"Perhaps today, you could teach Scáth and me what you know about the forest and its creatures?" Athvar was hesitant but could tell Ven genuinely wanted to learn, and most importantly, he wasn't like the other hunters or Kyst, for that matter. Athvar could sense a common trait between the two, and that was spontaneity, something Kysts absolutely lacked, which often made for uninteresting and hard-headed folk.

"Alright, today, I will share with ya what the forest will allow." Ven nodded and walked back to the rest of the party.

Several hours had gone by, and heavy rain had settled in. The party broke off into smaller groups, but Athvar stayed true to his promise and spent the day with Ven and Scáth. As the trio walked, Ven and Athvar taught her what they could. The Kyst was confident that if she could retain everything she learned over the hunt, she would be equipped to forage and brave the forest elements on her own if need be. At one point, Ven spotted a stag grazing in an open field. He went to knock an arrow, but Athvar put a hand up to stay the hunter.

"Ya said you wanted to learn. You can't do that if it is dead, can you, elf?" said the plucky little gnome. Scáth snickered with a smirk, and Ven reluctantly put his bow away. Soon, Athvar couldn't be spotted as he walked through the tall grass toward the stag. Ven almost pulled his bow out again when he noticed the stag suddenly taking a defensive stance. But before he knew it, Athvar was stroking the forehead of the beast, and what happened next shocked the ShadowScorn and Kyst equally. The stag bowed its head, lifting Athvar on his back, and the little gnome rode the animal over to the pair.

"Don't think because ya do not share a language that a connection cannot be established." Athvar was clearly proud as he approached them. Scáth couldn't believe the beauty of it up close. She gently placed her hand on his snout, to which the stag snorted excitedly. Ven had spent his entire life around such animals and had never known them to be so amiable. Of course, he had his encounters with the alpha wolf and SeaRaven but considered those to be connected to something else. However, Ven had to admit to himself that he could be wrong.

"If ya would, milady?" Athvar extended a hand to Scáth, who graciously helped the gnome off the nearly three-metre tall stag.

Athvar looked to Ven, who was still staring at the animal before him. "Get on," he said. Ven whipped his head toward the filthy gnome. "Ya said ya wanted to learn. If yar calm and yar mind is open, he will accept ya." Athvar was encouraging so Ven cautiously walked closer. Halfway to Ven's hand reaching his head, the stag dragged its hoof in the dirt and snorted.

"Remain calm and open," Athvar reminded.

"I am calm," Ven said defensively. The Kyst reached to close the distance, and the stag whipped his head back and then forth, connecting his antlers with Ven's torso. The hunter went flying through the field and gave a great yelp after landing on the ground. Scáth winced painfully on his behalf. Ven landed in extreme pain from his previous wounds reopening after the antler strike, his warrior instincts uncontrollable. He rolled, simultaneously knocking an arrow and loosed it into the eye of the stag. Scáth stepped back from being sprayed with blood. After the shock hit Athvar, he was about to verbally assault the daft and ignorant elf, yet much to Athvar's surprise, Ven beat him to it. The gnome and ShadowScorn were both shocked by the scream that echoed from Ven. A scream that evidently carried so much pain, confusion, sadness, and ultimately, unbridled anger. Scáth started to follow after Ven when he turned tail and vanished into the misty rainforest, but Athvar stopped her.

"Best he has some time to think on his own, eh." Athvar was trying to comfort Scáth, and though she appreciated it, her worry for Ven weighed heavily.

"Well, let's see about taking the stag back to camp," Scáth said at a loss for other words.

Ven walked in no particular direction until he stumbled upon a hot spring of turquoise mineral water. He gave a small thanks to Āina, for this beautiful spot. Though he wasn't sure why he did. Ven stripped off his clothes, save for his golden locket, and cleaned his wounds in the warm water. As he floated there in the steamy pool, surrounded by moss, beautiful birds, and tall trees, he felt the first sense of peace since finding that wounded bull elk. He moved from a state of floating to sinking until his back hit the bottom of the natural spring. This underwater meditation was common for Kyst, capable of holding their breath for such great lengths of time.

It wasn't until sometime later that Ven finally emerged from the pool floor. He immediately regretted it as he spotted—and more importantly, heard—the SeaRaven making a large commotion slightly overhead. When the bird landed on his gear, however, Ven remembered specifically asking it to "Keep an eye on things," and perhaps that's what was happening now. He scrambled to reach his equipment and dawn it quickly when he heard the snapping of twigs in the distance. Deciding he didn't have enough time, he threw the gear over his shoulder and scrambled up the nearest tree to dress and observe from above. After reaching a comfortable height, he put on his gear, and the SeaRaven landed on a branch beside him. Ven couldn't believe the damned bird had actually helped for once as three warriors walked by the pool.

"Wait," one of them said, putting his hand up for the trio to stop. Ven thought him to be a tracker of some kind. The ranger looked around the pool and noticed that water had recently been spilled over.

"What is it?" asked a woman wrapped in colourful robes that revealed much of her auburn skin.

"Something went from the water, up this tree," answered the ranger. Ven was literally holding his breath as the tracker amazingly followed a trail he hadn't even considered leaving.

"Or someone." The third warrior grunted. A two and a half metre tall hulking warrior in gleaming plate mail. He pulled his golden hood down to reveal something Ven had only ever read about. Dragon-bloods, massive humanoids with great horned heads, rows of razor-sharp teeth, strong scales, and deadly claws.

Ven, now fully dressed and aware that they were on to him, silently traversed a tree over to continue watching. "How did they even get onto the island?" he whispered to his SeaRaven. Although the island was surrounded by a thin beach and unscalable seacliffs, Ven was told there were only two access points. One being located near Hearth and the other secreted away.

Ven noticed the light-blue Dragon-blood breathing deeply with his eyes closed. Next thing the hunter knew, a ball of fire formed in the clawed hand, building momentum before shooting forth at the tree Ven had just leaped from. By the time the ball of fire reached its destination, it had grown exponentially and engulfed a large section of the branches. In truth, the hunter didn't give it as much thought as he should have. All he knew was that he loved the forest as much as life itself and would happily slaughter those who'd burn it so willingly. That rage he increasingly felt of late boiled over.

The three warriors stood there for a moment, watching the fire destroy most of the tree, when an arrow came soaring from above. The robed woman snapped out her arm with blinding speed to catch it just centimetres away from the Dragon-blood's head. The ranger deftly tucked behind a tree. Ven, even angrier by the stolen arrow, sent another into the foot of the woman, pinning her to the dirt. A great yelp was heard, and Ven noticed a crossbow bolt fly an arm's length away. The hunter nimbly walked out onto a branch to where he could see the ranger. One arrow was all it took to steal the life of that human as his body slumped against the tree.

The Dragon-blood yanked the arrow out of the woman's foot and carried her with one arm behind a collection of boulders. The half-dragon half-man walked back out into the open with his arms raised.

"Who are you?" yelled the hunter spewing outrage.

"I am one who spreads the word of Sesara, Goddess of life and sustenance, brother," replied the Dragon-blood with an air of attitude that Ven didn't favour.

"You are uninvited to this island. State your true intent and leave immediately."

"I offer no ill intent toward your people or the little ones. I seek but one fugitive to my land. Give her over and we shall leave peacefully."

"We're not on your land. She is a fugitive to nothing so long as she is under our watch. Now leave!" the hunter stated with utter enmity.

The large beastly humanoid responded with humour in his voice. "You do not know me, so I do not blame your ignorance."

Ven responded to that clear answer with an arrow rocketing toward his chest, but the arrow tip did not pierce, rather skipping off the impressive breastplate.

The Dragon-blood gave a great roar. "My Goddess protects me, Kyst elf! What do you have but the trees and brine?"

Just then, Ven heard the familiar caw of his SeaRaven and saw the bird clawing at the Holy Warrior's eyes. Ven leaped from the tree, extending his trident as he fell. The SeaRaven stopped just as Ven drove the trident deep into the Dragon-blood's chest, rolling forward and off. Ven stood up and turned around to see an already dead monstrosity. As he stood up he got the shock of a lifetime as the Dragon-blood stood up as well, removing the bloody trident and throwing it aside.

With blood spewing from his massive craw, he said, "I told you my deity protects me," and lunged full speed toward Ven. He didn't have time to respond before he was picked up by the neck and thrown bodily backwards, rolling uncontrollably until the ground ended his inertia. Ven rolled over slowly to support himself on his forearms, shaking off the dizziness that followed. The Dragon-blood was already on him, lifting him by the neck with both claws and strangling Ven against a tree. He struggled against the pressure, trying to squeeze his fingers between the Dragon-blood's talons to prevent him from snapping his neck.

"Fear not, pagan. I will cleanse this world of all ShadowScorn, thus fulfilling the test placed before us by our mother, Sesara."

Ven's green eyes winced at the thought of this beast getting anywhere near Scáth. Fearing to let one hand go to grab a weapon for even a second would end with the cracking of his neck, he thought there was little choice left. He dropped one hand behind his waist, drew his short sword and drove it into the side of the Warriors neck. The Dragon-blood opened his razor-sharp mouth wide in an effort to consume Ven's face. The hunter could literally see his blade in the back of his throat, ultimately this did nothing but aid Ven in cutting off the warrior's head.

Dropped to his knees, the elf knelt by the tree for a moment rubbing his quickly bruising neck.

"This has been a week," he said, coughing. Then came a rather seductive and feminine voice.

"Well, it isn't over yet, honey," said the colourfully robed woman who managed to catch Ven's first arrow. He instantly noticed she was not limping on the wounded foot as it appeared already completely healed. Ven cleared his throat, stood up, cracking his neck, asking,

"What's your deal then? Because he was cleansing ShadowScorn." Ven pointed to the Dragon-blood with its head hanging on only by a few stubborn scales. He then wiped the purple blood off his sword on the golden hood.

"I'm more of an old-school Sesara kind of gal. Not one for killing the innocent, alas, you did just murder one of our ranking paladins."

"Generally 'murder' is reserved for those who were undeserving of death," Ven responded dryly.

"All the same, honey. I'd make peace with yourself now." The woman bowed lavishly and waited in a readied stance. Ven wasn't surprised to see she carried no weapons. Monks were masters of the martial arts, and he always admired them for their skill and sheer discipline. Though he never guessed this would be how his first encounter with one would go. He dropped his bow and quiver, then removed his cloak. She gave him a smirk. Ven replaced the short sword with a throwing dagger in each hand. At this point, his body was barely holding together, but he had trained his entire life to put that in the back of his mind.

She came in with a flurry of punches, to which Ven responded adequately enough to block. She fed him enough jabs to the head until he was blocking high enough to leave his mid-section exposed, to which she delivered a devastating kick to his abdomen. Ven stumbled back, almost keeling over to vomit.

She did not cease. Ven was back defending an almost blur of punches and kicks in a matter of seconds. The two were in a calculated and lightening fast dance with each other. Ven blocked one punch with his forearm and managed to spin his blade around, slicing the back of her elbow deeply. To which she instantly responded with a spinning kick to his head, followed by a series of direct punches to his kidneys. Ven lazily swung his dagger around, but she nimbly avoided the attack altogether. Ven managed to work some distance between the two as he caught his breath. She, however, was looking able and willing to fight for hours.

"When I prepared to come here, everyone told me to watch out for the Kyst. Truthfully, I think your reputation has outgrown your strength." When she said that, it occurred to Ven, even by the way she was dressed, that the forest was not her traditional environment. It was bumpy, muddy, and unpredictable terrain that had risen in elevation over thousands of years of loose decomposing flora. So Ven took the offensive, pressing the fight in the direction of his choosing. Swinging his daggers and jabbing in a manner that kept the monk on her toes and constantly in a state of dodge and weave. Soon Ven found an area that had soil erosion, exposing many of the long and tangled roots of these mighty trees. Ven threw one dagger, and the monk rolled low and backwards, causing the dagger to miss and then springing back up to avoid a swing with Ven's short sword. He threw the other dagger. This time, she caught and threw it back into his thigh. As soon as she let go of the dagger, her heel caught a root, and she tumbled backwards. She instinctually rolled with the fall, and Ven awaiting the move, threw his short sword directly into her chest as she began to exit it.

A deep gasp escaped her as she sat on the wet ground. Ven relaxed from his throwing stance and walked a little closer, still cautious of his opponent.

"You were an admirable foe. I do hope your God welcomes you with a warm embrace," Ven offered with conviction. The monk woman breathed her last breath and he removed his short sword from her chest and the dagger from her leg. He wasted no time in collecting the Dragon-blood's head and his glove that had the symbol of Sesara on it.

It was just after dark by the time Ven returned to camp. The party was enjoying their dinner when he snuck upon them. He dropped the large head and glove on the ground.

Everyone reacted in predictable shock, and all that could be heard was the nighttime forest.

"What happened to you?" Scáth quickly got up but not in time to catch the hunter before he fell to the ground, overtaken by his wounds once more.

CHAPTER SIX

Dark Tidings

Several days had gone by since Ven awoke from his dramatic entrance into camp. Athvar and Tolmie quickly went to stabilize the hunter, even so far as to brew him a herbal medicine that allowed for extended sleep. The Kyst opened his opalescent eyes that appeared to somehow reflect every shade of green. Seeing Scáth seated in a chair next to a window and a roaring fireplace, he felt a sense of comfort overcome him and thought he even spotted snow outside.

"Milady," his voice strained. She looked at the hunter with excitement and moved to sit on the edge of the bed. She brushed a long lock of hair from his eye.

"Good sir," she whispered back. Ven sat up in bed feeling more rested than wounded with his previous injuries finally allowed the time necessary to heal. He looked out the window with squinty eyes, and she followed his gaze.

"First snowfall." She looked back at him. "Thank you for protecting me, again."

"It's not safe here for you anymore," he promptly stated.

"Of course it is. You are here," she said reassuringly, trying to calm the Kyst.

"I didn't stop anything the first time. Or the second and this last confrontation was on a different scale. They were all highly skilled warriors. One of them wielded immense power, bestowed upon him by his Goddess." Ven clearly wasn't taking no for an answer this time.

It was obvious if someone did want to get on the island badly enough, they could. He did, however, intend on learning how these three found passage onto Sanctuary Island. Scáth looked at him, unsure why he was giving himself such sparse credit.

"Has Vakar been by?" he sheepishly asked while swinging his legs out of bed, planting his feet firmly. The ShadowScorn just shook her head slightly, causing the billowing ends of her hair to mist away in a wide pattern. Ven gave half a nod before springing up and began to dawn his armour and weapons.

"What are you doing?"

"Come on, I want to hear what Ilthanis and Tolmie have decided what should be done," he said while strapping his short sword to his lower back. Scáth just shrugged, undeniably inclined to also find out what the wise and intelligent leaders of this island would suggest. The pair left the cabin in a hurry, walking toward town hall, where they hoped to find someone who could prepare the meeting. Scáth approached the deeply voiced gnome who had previously delivered Ven's bamboo attire. Much to the hunter's surprise, the gnome was cheery and jovial when talking to the ShadowScorn. After a moment of chatter, the gnome went off and Scáth returned.

"He asked for us to wait inside," she said, grinning.

"Why are you smiling so?" he questioned as they walked up to the doors.

"He was worried you aren't actually the 'Mighty Ven Devar' and perhaps just someone who gets hurt all the time." Ven just rolled his eyes as Scáth gave a little giggle. The hall felt empty and dim, echoing the small disturbances created by his movement. The two sat down next to each other at the table in the back.

"Do you feel ready to begin the journey home?" She could understand from the inflection in his voice that Ven was serious.

"I am," her words layered in confidence.

"Good, then let's see to our immediate departure," the Kyst replied definitively. A minute later, Queen Ilthanis walked inside along with Tolmie. Ilthanis quickly outpaced the little gnome with clear intent.

"It's such a relief to my soul seeing you up and well, Ven Devar." She gave a bow uncharacteristic to one of her station.

"Worry not, Your Highness. Just a slight hiccup in an otherwise successful hunt. It was a true pleasure working so closely with the

Gnomes of Hearth." Ven looked to Tolmie and gave him a casual wink. Tolmie's face brightened to see the hunter was in such good spirits and health.

"I must admit, Ven. I didn't think yee'd be calling a meetin' so soon after yer sleep, but it surely brightened our day!" Tolmie proclaimed in his usual boisterous and affable way. Ven just smiled, allowing Scáth to speak.

"We were most eager to hear your wisdom." She finished with a demeanour poised to listen. Ilthanis and Tolmie took their seats across from the duo. The queen thought they made a good team and had much to learn from each other.

"I'm pleased to hear that, Lady Scáth," Ilthanis kindly offered. "I believe the two of us have reached an accord that should benefit all." Ven looked from the queen to Scáth, who seemed so regal and comfortable in this setting. His attention was jolted back to the queen once he heard his name.

"Ven, I propose you instate me as temporary ruler of Silva's people. This will allow us to achieve Trilara's final wishes with utmost efficiency. You will take, Scáth back to her homeland, and the Sages of Hearth and Silva may begin rebuilding the once marvellous place." The queen spoke with clear transparency, open to any suggestions the duo may have.

"Athvar has even offered to accompany the two of yee to ShadowScorn," added Tolmie. Ven couldn't believe that news. He thought Athvar would never wish to see him again after his outburst during the hunt. He didn't say anything, lost in thought. So Scáth filled the air once more.

"It would be a most wonderful thing to have Athvar 'The Undusted' join us."

Tolmie laughed aloud. "Then it's settled!"

"Pardon me, Your Highness, but where is Vakar in all this?" Ven cut through Tolmie and Scáth's conversation.

"He has taken it upon himself to lead the regrowth and rebuilding of Silva. He is with the other sages as we speak," she replied evenly. "He has been of unparalleled help since the disaster of your people."

"And does that not seem odd to you? He lost everything, including his betrothed."

"Everyone reacts to tragedy differently," the queen replied evenly.

Ven looked to Scáth again, who returned the glance. While still looking at Scáth, he declared, "Then it is settled, Queen Ilthanis is the ruler until my return. Scáth and I will prepare to leave in the morning." Ven looked back to Ilthanis. "But I will have words with Vakar before we depart." The four gave signs of respect to one another and left the hall.

Scáth and Ven walked through town and stopped to look at the beautiful view of the Northern Archipelago.

"Please tell me what is on your mind, Ven?" Scáth asked earnestly. They stood in silence as Ven thought how best to articulate his worries.

"Vakar and I have known each other for more of our life than not. It doesn't surprise me he has handled this so well, yet the fact everyone overlooks is his misplacing of the blame for what happened."

"On you?" she asked.

"Yes." It sounded sharper than he intended. "He's a genius if there ever was one. A great Kyst, but can be petty and vengeful to his core."

"Everyone knows you two are like brothers. Surely he will understand and agree it is best to move forward." Although she didn't seem to be convincing Ven otherwise, she thought it was best to remind him of something positive. "I will speak to Athvar about gathering the right supplies for our journey. You make things right with Vakar." She planted a quick kiss on the Kyst's greyish cheek. Ven's eyes widened, and a stupid look crossed his face. Before he could respond, Scáth was gracefully and as always, silently walking away. He shook the adolescent and excited look off his face. Ven walked through the rest of Hearth until reaching the only building that was constructed from logged trees. It was of utterly extravagant design, with large carved statues of Kyst sages overlooking the entrance.

Ven walked through the mighty doors to find a classy and austere interior. A large walkway with doors off-shooting it surrounded a lower area on all sides. These rooms were separated by a short flight of stairs. At the bottom of those stairs was a massive cedar slab table bedecked with maps, books, and scattered papers, as ten ornately-robed sages frantically debated amongst each other.

Ven thought it strange that no one noticed him enter but remembered these elves lived to be lost in their work. They were of the most intelligent, wise, and ingenious Kyst ever born and arguably the most scholarly elves in Litore. In a way, polar opposites to their counterparts, the hunters. Yet both complimented the other beautifully when working together. Ven cleared his throat while approaching the table, which caught the attention of several sages. All recognizing instantly the conversation about to transpire, quickly went to vacating the common area into separate rooms located on the upper walkway. By the time Ven was next to Vakar—who still had his back turned to him—there was only one other sage left in the room. After a moment, Vakar and this sage stopped talking. The sage collected his things and paused to give Ven an unimpressed and rather hostile glance. The hunter met it without any emotion, denying the catty sage any enjoyment.

"Good to see you, Vakar," Ven said hopefully. Vakar still faced the other way looking at papers scattered on the table.

"Indeed. How do you fair?" he asked with little interest.

"Fine. Ilthanis is our temporary ruler now. I hope that settles well with you." Although Ven couldn't see Vakar's reaction, the sage was wearing a large grin. Vakar turned around with a now sincere look.

"I think that is the right course of action, brother. Then you are off to escort Lady Scáth home?" Vakar said with what seemed like genuine care.

"Yes. I will be back early next spring if all goes well," Ven said firmly, expecting some flak or snide remark.

Vakar replied with a smile. "The sages and I will have regrown most of Silva's trees by then. You will be back just in time for the important work." Ven thought his friend seemed a tad too keen all of a sudden.

"I leave the rebuilding of Silva in your capable hands." The hunter pulled the ancient royal artifact out from under his armour, tugged it free, and handed it to Vakar.

"We've been over this…" Vakar was cut off by Ven aggressively grabbing his wrist and speaking loudly.

"It may very well be that I'm not fated to survive the journey. Perhaps a feral will rip our throats out and eat us whole, or my soul devoured by a Syphon and my husk left to roam the land as a horrid monster. Either way, this artifact must remain with the people of Silva." Ven slapped the necklace into Vakar's hand and closed his fingers tightly, pushing the sage's arm back while doing so.

"Goodbye, ol'friend." Ven hugged Vakar, who echoed in response.

"Goodbye, ol'friend." The two shared a brief hug, and Ven left with haste. He thought it was unceremonious at best, but if he put his cynical side to the back, he considered it went well enough. It truly wouldn't be that long, and then Ven would submit himself to his bestowed upon duties. Vakar watched Ven walk away with a grimace.

CHAPTER SEVEN

Adventure Awaits

Ven sat with a loose hanging blanket over his bare skin in front of the fireplace throughout the whole night, meditating. The locket of Renic hung around his neck to lay against his sternum, acted as a metaphysical anchor during these sessions. He had simple white tattoos on the inside of his wrists, the round of his shoulders, and down his mid-centre. The Kyst all sported natural tattoos of varying colours and designs.

There is little doubt in my mind that I am skilled enough for the task that lay ahead of Scáth, Athvar, and me. Nevertheless, this will mark my first time departing the Northern Rainforest's reach. I've spent many years patrolling our borders and have seen the wicked vileness that trickles over. Bandits that would no sooner cut your throat and rob you than a beast would tear your insides out to feed her young. It is a cruel and impartial world. I mustn't forget my ancestors fled to this very spot in search of a more peaceful realm. ShadowScorn is to the south of Litore's highest peak, Moon Mountain. We will travel off of but along the Great Road for as long as we can. Nobody does or should trust anybody along most of the Great Road, as it's seldom patrolled by a nearby kingdom or city. Opportunistic folk call the Great Road home, and it would appear Scáth is a walking king's ransom for anyone willing to take her to Serenstrom. Going along the northern edge of the Morass Prairie and down Litore Lake is the quickest route but predictably the most dangerous. Athvar suggests planning as we go, I often defer to experience and wiser voices during times such as these.

***

-Ven Devar

Ven was awake before the first light, gearing up for the first true adventure of his life. He intended on seeing to Scáth's continued training in survival and, if time permitting, combat. He had considered that with her ability to blend in with the shadow around her, she could, with time, become a fierce warrior, or rogue as they were often referred to. He was caught mid-thought as he spotted the glint of his SeaRaven's eye against the moon outside his window. He took a deep breath before leaving his cabin, then proceeded to meet Scáth and Athvar in the town square.

"Rise and shine, elf! A new day of adventure and intrigue awaits!" Athvar exclaimed and went to pumping his little legs toward the trail down to the water. Ven stopped beside Scáth to watch the gnome enthusiastically walk off. She put a casual hand on his shoulder.

"Should we always give him a head start?" Ven asked sarcastically. Scáth laughed a little louder than intended, and the pair followed after the gnome. On the way down, Ven handed Scáth a large wrapped gift.

"Something I thought you might need for our trip." He handed it to her with a smile. Scáth took it graciously, quickly and excitedly opened it. It revealed a dense black cloak with curled grey waves embroidered on the trim as accents. It was made from the same infamously warm and durable wool of the PumaSheep.

"How you spoil me, Ven Devar. Thank you." She gently squeezed his hand before she donned the magnificent cloak and hood.

Two local Kyst from Hearth were waiting at the beach with a small fishing boat ready to ferry them to the mainland. They sailed the trio under a fresh golden sky around the eastern end of Sanctuary Island. It was early afternoon by the time they found themselves in a cove along the Litores mainland coast. They decided it would be best if they avoided Silva and spent the first day walking east along the coastline. Any snow that remained was quickly washed away by heavy rain that came with the early evening. Athvar and Scáth went to hang a piece of canvas that could slope the rain away from their heads. Ven, however, went fishing with his trident. As he sat on the shoreline, in the pouring rain, cleaning a SharkSalmon for dinner. Athvar and Scáth sat comfortably next to a fire and couldn't help but be slightly impressed by Ven's love of being in nature. Unbothered by the elements, content on land or sea and capable of thriving in both. While Ven had been fishing, Athvar and Scáth collected a dinner of mushrooms, lichen, and varying vegetables. It wasn't long before the trio was stuffed, seated contently around the fire, listening to the rain impact the world around them. Soon Scáth was asleep, nestled tightly in her new cloak and blanket. Ven noticed Athvar holding a stare on him. Without turning his head to meet the gaze, he stated blankly,

"Ask if you wish to ask, but stop staring at me, little man." Athvar didn't seem all too laughable.

"First off, don't compare gnomes to men. It's rude." He looked at the hunter with his large brown eyes. "Secondly, you're afraid. I deserve to know why."

Ven figured it truly didn't matter and was happy to disclose his concerns.

"I've never left the rainforest, and I have a feeling my closest comrade in life is up to something despicable. Even worse, I just left him to his own devices to escort someone I barely know thousands of kilometres across Litore, not forgetting we're also just in time for winter's renewal."

Slowly but surely, a wide grin crossed Athvar's dusty face.

"I've travelled every main stretch of the Great Road and seen many wonders along the way. I assure ya, we'll see ShadowScorn soon enough. As for yar comrade problem, it's times like these I'm thankful for being a simple gnome. Ya elves live such exhaustive and extensive lives."

"I am grateful for your joining us, Athvar. Thank you." Athvar nodded kindly in return and looked over to Scáth.

"Truthfully, there is something about the girl that pulled me toward the journey." Ven hadn't heard the gnome speak so openly before.

"She is intoxicating, isn't she?" Ven knew Scáth had an aura of care and gentleness. He thought it was a quality most folk picked up on.

"Good night, Ven Devar." Athvar rolled on his side and cuddled closely with his chipmunk companion. Ven sat with his back against a tree, wrapped up in his cloak. With his SeaRaven fluttering above, he decided to rest for a few hours.

* * *

When he woke up in the morning to Scáth saying his name, it became clear his wounds were still demanding rest.

"Come on, elf, we cut through the forest past Claw Canyon today," Athvar exclaimed in his usual upbeat attitude. Ven just put up a hand to silence the gnome and nodded in agreeance.

"I can only assume you know who calls Claw Canyon home, Athvar?" queried Ven rhetorically.

"Of course! So we better not dilly'dattle less'n we end up as leathers for some Kintar raider," Athvar managed to joke about the horrible and all too real fate. Scáth immediately flicked her head to Ven.

"What!" she shrieked in outrage. Ven looked to Athvar, stunned, then looked back to Scáth and blurted out.

"He's just having fun. Right, Athvar?" Ven was clearly trying to hint at something to the gnome. Alas, Athvar remained unaware.

"Oh no, it's as real as Chips here." The chipmunk on his shoulder responded with a loud squeak. "I mean, Chips would probably be fine, but I'd most likely end up as a coat for some Kintar child." The gnome felt less and less funny as his sentence went on, and looked up to Scáth, who appeared horrified, and Ven shaking his head with frustration.

"But they're known for ceasing raids this time of year and stay in the Canyon. So nothin' to fear Lady Scáth." The ShadowScorn just took a deep breath and accepted this was the reality she was faced with for now. Something Ven noticed and admired for her being able to do. An ability he himself struggled with.

The trio left without a trace and headed south through the rainforest. The steady downpour was accompanied by winter's first intense brisk air, threatening to turn to snow at any time. The hunter could be sure it was already snowing at higher elevations, but that wouldn't be a worry till they were safely past Claw Canyon. It was several hours into their days-trek when they heard the first skin-crawling Roar of Kintar in the distance. Ven watched as Scáth and Athvar both threw themselves down into the large ferns and fallen thicket. The hunter knew them to be far off and ushered his jittery friends forward.

Soon another Kintar howl was heard, then another, and another. It became evident quickly that the trio was surrounded by unassuming packs of roaming raiders. Ven quickened his pace momentarily to begin leading them through what he could determine would be the safest route. The Kintar were anything but graceful. Great Grizzly bears could and would make less noise and disturbance to the area surrounding them. For that reason, this Kyst and his superlative senses found some degree of ease in circumnavigating the noisy packs of lumbering raiders. The three adventures thought they had safely manoeuvred between the troops of Kintar until Ven almost stepped directly through a bush off a ten-metre embankment into a heavily occupied camp. He felt his stomach lurch as his foot gave way on the edge of the bank. Falling forward now, he looked upon the camp and felt his hood get yanked on by Scáth. The hunter was skinnier than most Kyst, but this allowed him greater speed, agility in combat, as well as an easier time ascending trees. Thankfully, Scáth was stronger than she looked and heaved Ven back toward them. A large clump of soil that gave way with Ven's foot went tumbling down the bank, catching the attention of a few Kintar cooking a charred humanoid arm over a fire nearby.

All three of the companions looked at each other with wide eyes and shock. Ven was a darker shade of grey as he felt so very stupid, but Scáth and Athvar knew they both would have made the same mistake. For the bushes that grew along the ridge of the embankment appeared as any other route would in the forest. Scáth quickly put her hand to her mouth when she heard the voices of three brutish raiders talking at the bottom of the hill. Ven was versed in the tongue of these elves, a similar dialect to Kystin but more guttural, knew them to be fighting each other about needing to investigate further. Soon Ven heard all the commotion stop as the Kintar below started aggressively sniffing the wind. Athvar noticed Scáths beautiful misting hair billowing toward the camp.

"We must go quickly," whispered the little gnome with worry. Ven nodded his head, and the trio was off with haste.

Much to everyone's relief, they had managed to pass Claw Canyon and any Kintar by day's end. Ven managed to survey a cave formed by a giant boulder slide. It had a thick layer of moss coating it and a well-used trail leading inside.

Ven looked at Athvar through the heavy rain as it soaked them better than jumping in the ocean would have. "You wanna inquire about the inhabitants?"

Athvar didn't say anything though. Chips popped out of his pocket and scurried into his hand. The two stared at each other for a brief moment, then Chips just gave what Ven could only assume was a nod to the gnome and scurried toward the cave entrance. Athvar just looked confidently at the pair and then watched his buddy do his work. Chips was gone for a long-time, and Ven assumed he had become a snack for the occupant of the cave. Shortly thereafter, the chipmunk came sprinting out of the cave with determination. Athvar and his tiny friend shared another silent moment before turning to look at Ven and Scáth happily.

"We're set! Ya just have to give her fish, and she'll let us stay the night."

Scáth smiled widely and fluttered her eyes in confusion. "What?"

"Yes, what?" added Ven almost immediately after.

Athvar didn't understand the holdup. "Chips made a deal for us, ya just have to give'r a fish is all! C'mon." And with that, Athvar and Chips waddled their way inside out of the harsh elements. Scáth and Ven shrugged, hesitantly following a comfortable distance behind. Upon entering, they were barraged with a pungent stench, and Scáth went to pinching her nose.

"Good luck holding your nose all night. Even I can't hold my breath that long," Ven said jokingly, moving ahead of Scáth as the cave narrowed before opening into a larger den. It was just as Ven expected after the smell, a two-ton Grizzly bear all nested in for the beginning of hibernation. Scáth was predictably taken aback at first, but she warmed up to the idea after she saw Athvar and Chips already snuggled up to the bear. Ven took out a fish that was tightly wrapped in leaves and fed it whole to the Grizzly. He looked to Athvar while the bear ate from his hand.

"How do you speak with Chips?"

"A form of communication can as always be established. For starters, this Grizzly is going to like ya a lot more now." Athvar motioned to the Grizzly, who was now licking her massive snout before giving a wet and stinky kiss across the Kyst's whole face. Ven laughed and responded by placing his forehead on the bears.

Scáth slowly walked over to the furry and beautiful animal, giving her a few pets. She then tip-toed next to Athvar and Chips and promptly found a spot to get comfortable. As the stunning

ShadowScorn lay there in the cave, cuddled up with a gnome and a chipmunk against a Grizzly bear, she admitted to herself that she was lucky. To have found such entrusting companions and friends. She thought she was beginning to enjoy this life of travel and adventure, albeit strange and unpredictable.

CHAPTER EIGHT
A New Pack

In the northern sub-tropical rainforest, a few days from Silva, lay a heaping mass of black fur with white spots that undeniably resembled a night sky. He was curled tightly in a pile of ferns, with his snout tucked neatly under his tail to maintain as much heat as possible on these cold nights alone. Tired and weary from fighting alongside the Kyst hunter he felt so attached to. Swimming the great distance from the mainland to Sanctuary Island, left the wolf physically exhausted. He hadn't had any luck with hunting since the decimation of his pack at the hands of the Kintar ambush. He knew all too well that if food couldn't be found soon, he may not survive the winter. The once 250-kilogram canine had lost nearly a fifth of that weight in the last few weeks.

Two ears shot up from the otherwise indistinguishable mass of fur. The occasional snapping of branches and scraping of bark could be heard not far off. The alpha arose from his shallow hole to gain a better perception of his surroundings. From what he could hear, it sounded as though a stag was rubbing its antlers against a tree. He slowly put one wide paw in front of the other as he stalked his way closer to the sound. The forest was still dark, with the rising sun not yet outshining the thick canopy. Perfect conditions for the predator. Carefully calculating every step in front of him to make the least amount of sound possible, letting his ears and nose guide his direction. This majestic beast was, without doubt, a special animal, graceful, intelligent, and blessed with the penultimate apex-predator form of strength and dexterity. As proven with his ability to sneak up on Ven, his size did nothing to diminish his stealth as the stag, indeed aggressively scraping his antlers against a tree, came into view. The wolf came up behind his prey, unnoticed. Slowly and patiently, stalking with his head hung low. The stag, seemingly unaware of the danger lurking behind him, stopped a moment, looking off in a random direction. The alpha sprang, with all his might, easily clearing the six-metre gap to land on the back of the deer. The stag gave a bellow and began bucking. But the hulking wolf had already clamped his jaw onto the snout, and before long, they tumbled into mildew-covered grass. On the ground, the wolf began sporadically biting the deer's neck and digging with his claws into the belly of his prey. Before long, the alpha was enjoying the heat of his food warming his belly. Eventually, he dragged the carcass to his spot on the forest floor. Savouring the carcass so he could have several meals and attempt to regain some lost mass.

    The day came and went for the wolf, who was content in his small burrow. That night, however, he found less peace. The wolf curled up again tightly and was awoken by a howl echoing through the trees. This time, however, the wolf immediately leaped up in a defensive and aggressive stance, with teeth bared and hackles taught. Then another howl came from the creature but much closer. He was familiar with the howl travelling through the air. It was that of the unnatural Feral. Humanoid creatures that had willingly undergone dark and gruesome transformations to become animalistic in physical form. The wolf however only knew these creatures as dangerous and unpredictable. For the howl, he heard this night was that of a werewolf, and it was fast approaching. Sooner than anticipated, the long finger-like claws of the werewolf gripped the edge of a tree. It slowly revealed its head with a drooling snarl, displaying a disgusting mixture of human and canine teeth. Its snout was long and came to a sharper point, with patchy bits of black hair covering its human-like skin. The beast stood over two metres tall and could run just as fast as any wolf. The alpha didn't care if he met his end here, for the very existence of a Feral was a mockery of nature and therefore must die.

    They both howled with everything they could muster, and the alpha sprinted into action. The werewolf came around the tree and kicked with supernatural speed, but the wolf predicted the move. Ducking to the side to avoid the kick, the alpha bit hard on the monster's other leg and kept running. Forcing the feral to hit the ground and be dragged for a short distance. Before long, it reared its free leg into the side of the alpha, causing him to lose his grip and go hurdling to the side. The wolf did half a dozen barrel roles before getting back on all four paws. By the time he regained stability, the feral was already advancing. The alpha leaped off a dead log to body slam his foe but instead was batted aside. The alpha was used to being the strongest and knew he would have to change up his strategy. Before he had the chance, he felt the excruciating bite on his front right leg as the werewolf chomped down. The alpha gave a loud yelp of pain and bit hard on the feral's long snout. The alpha was being swung through the air with his hind legs kicking to find ground. All the while, the werewolf was swiping his deadly and long claws against the alpha's body, finding purchase several times. The wolf deciding he couldn't drag the beast down, changed his tactic again. Still clamping hard on the snout of the monster, tasting blood now, the alpha dug his hind legs into the werewolf's belly and his front claws into his shoulders. Then pushed as hard as he could while pulling on the snout with all the strength in his thick neck. He quickly heard the increased whimpers and frantic movements coming from the feral. Then the wolf felt a release of pressure, and the entire head of the werewolf separated in the alpha's mouth. The alpha wolf, still king of this forest, gave a long and powerful howl atop the dead feral. Tired and beaten, the alpha went back to his burrow for rest.

    The next morning he ate another large meal from the stag before he had caught the scent of a flock of PumaSheep. The wolf knew if he bided his time, he could catch one of the much smaller creatures alone. Or, at the very least, he could scavenge what they had left behind from their kills. A PumaSheep averaged fifty kilograms and had thick coats of woodland fur. They were tightly wound with muscle and had great jaws with teeth designed for shredding. The wolf considered it to be his best option for food and left his burrow, following the scent.

It was the fifth day of the trio's journey, and they knew they would be near the Great Road within the next three days. Ven halted the group as he looked upwards into thick canopy of twisting branches and dangling vines.

"What is it?" whispered Scáth, who had sidled right behind the hunter.

"PumaSheep in the tree over there. They never travel alone."

"Are you sure, elf? I don't see it," Athvar chimed in, just as proficient in the wild as the Kyst. Ven just nodded in response. PumaSheep were experts at not being seen, however, this hunter had trained relentlessly to spot such things.

"Scáth, don't turn your back to this one." Ven pointed toward the animal sitting in the tree.

"Okay," she said confidently, although truthfully, she could not spot it either. The hunter slowly turned to look behind them and noticed two more PumaSheep crouching in the bushes. Athvar did however spot those two shortly after Ven.

"Don't suppose you speak with them, do you?" asked Ven quietly.

"Tried that once, learned me lesson," Athvar moved the dusty collar from his neck to reveal a nasty scar in the shape of a bite mark.

"Keep facing these two. There are more. I know it." Ven turned away to survey what he could. He counted six more and could safely assume there was another handful somewhere.

"Scáth," Ven prompted.

"Yes?"

"Pull out your scimitar." As he said this, Ven unclipped his trident from his right hip with his left hand. His right hand went behind his waist to grab his short sword and held them out defensively. Ven noticed Athvar dipping his pointed mace in a green fluid he had pulled from his pouch. The trio stood still, waiting for the next move. Ven watched as the PumaSheep in the tree stood up and leaped straight down at him. He fell to his back, compressing his knees and kicked up at the PumaSheep. As the creature went flying down a small berm behind the trio, everything broke loose.

The wolf had been trailing the flock at a fair distance for the past few days. He heard things erupt around the same time he caught the familiar scent of Ven and Scáth. He perked his ears up and dashed through the trees to reach the fight.

Athvar was charged by the two he had been having a staring contest with. They both leaped at the gnome in unison but overestimated his height. Athvar crouched, lifting his mace to let it scrap the belly of one PumaSheep. Before it could turn around again to pounce once more, it hit the ground, fast asleep. Scáth swung wide and hard as one jumped at her, claws poised for her chest. Her scimitar, impossibly sharp and light, easily cut one of the creature's paws off, forcing it into an unbalanced crash. Ven followed through on his roll after kicking the PumaSheep away and was instantly defending off three more of the creatures. Each one nipped and swiped at his feet, creating a semi-circle around him. To make things worse, he saw Athvar get tackled by one of the PumaSheep and lost sight of the gnome in some tall thicket. Ven was pinned by the creatures, unable to move where he wanted, for it was all he could do to prevent them from biting him. He threw his trident into the side of one, skewering it, but another PumaSheep just took its place. Ven thought he had failed once more and for the very last time when he heard Scáth scream as one PumaSheep clamped onto her wrist. She was flailing in every way to get this creature that bit her sword arm off, but it was holding tight. Ven threw a dagger while swinging at his own foes, it connected with the hip of the creature attacking Scáth but did nothing to stop it. Just as Ven was about to sacrifice an opportunity for the PumaSheep to bite him so he could get to Scáth, a massive form came soaring through the trees. Cleanly taking the creature off Scáth and tearing its throat out in the process. Ven was reinvigorated at his returned companion and unleashed a whirlwind of attacks, expertly placing each short sword strike.

"Find the gnome!" Ven yelled to the wolf, who responded by running over to Athvar's last known location. Ven rushed over to Scáth and grabbed her scimitar on the way. He firmly placed it in her hand and grabbed her wrist to examine the wound. He was astonished at the little damage that was done. Yes, there was an obvious wound he clearly saw, but she was barely bleeding, and the puncture marks were inconsistent with what should have happened. He looked at her with wide eyes and she truly didn't know how to explain it.

"Look out!" she yelled while pointing at two more PumaSheep closing in. Ven swiftly turned around with sword extended, slicing one almost in two. The second one immediately tackled the hunter, and they tumbled to the side, with the PumaSheep coming out on top.

Ven had his thick leather bracer in the mouth of the creature but knew it wouldn't last long before those fangs found flesh. The aggressive jolt to his body caused him to lose grip of his short sword, so he pulled a dagger from a small sheath on his ribs and drove it into the neck of the beast. The PumaSheep went still, and Ven rolled it off of him. With at least a dozen dead around them, Scáth and Ven found themselves in a quiet forest again. The Kyst looked all around for the wolf and gnome. The alpha came lumbering through the ferns with Athvar safely secured on his back, the gnome clearly adoring the experience. When Ven had finished wrapping Scáth's wound, he gave the alpha a tight hug around his neck.

"Fine companion you have here, elf!" Athvar exclaimed, sitting comfortably on the wolf's back. Scáth standing away from the rest looked slightly stunned by the wolf's return. Ven waved to her with a heartwarming smile, beckoning her to join. She took a shaky step toward the alpha, who now patiently sat. She was reminded of that nightmare of an evening when she was almost torn to shreds and devoured by this very wolf and his pack. Nevertheless, she walked toward them with determination. She gently placed her pale hand on the alpha's furry neck. He responded in kind with a long lick up her forearm.

CHAPTER NINE
Evil in the Night

I am often reminded that fate is a funny thing. The wolf who saved Scáth from a gruesome end at the claws of PumaSheep had also tried to kill the ShadowScorn a few weeks prior. I am still very lost as to why the alpha was putting itself through such dangers to protect me. Athvar insisted the wolf travel with us for as long as possible, and for the next few days, it seemed he would stick around for a while. As we reach the edge of the rainforest, I constantly wonder what he will do, surely it would mark his first exit from the forest, just as it will mine. He proved an excellent sentry during the previous nights, which has lifted a great strain from my state of mind. I already admit to myself how much I care for his well-being. As I know he cares for mine, perhaps even Scáth and Athvar's as well. I do not forget that I have undeniably saved this wolf's life once and he has saved mine twice. Taking a ferry was also a first for the wolf as we did today, cutting our travel time by two days instead of going around Sitka Sound. It was a novel experience for all the Halfling ferry workers, getting to see the colossal wolf casually travelling with us. I can feel a certain sense of relief from Scáth as we get ever closer to the forest's edge. However, I fear the open world to be a far more dangerous place than the land of trees.

-Ven Devar

The forest began to brighten, and a stronger breeze could be felt as the tree line gave way to the edge of the Morass Prairie. A land of rolling hills, prickly thicket, and tall grass as far as the eye can see. Mixed in were vast mires of scum-layered water and swampy creatures with never enough food. The party would travel between the edge of the prairie, next to and along the Great Road for as long as possible. However, Scáth was making sure Athvar and Ven were aware of what a target she would present out in the open.

As the trio founds the border of the forest, Ven looked back to see if the wolf would follow. He halted to watch his companion sniffing frantically all around the new terrain. Occasionally glancing up to scan the open horizon. The group admired the Three Moons, being shown in a different light against the cloud brushed, pale blue sky. Scáth went back the short distance to the edge of the forest and knelt beside the wolf. She placed her hand on his head and leaned against the majestic animal who fully supported her resting weight.

"Thank you, Faenla." Scáth kissed him between his eyes, where two white spots resembled four pointed stars. She stood up and walked back toward Ven and Athvar.

The trio had walked barely a minute before the wolf snuck his head between Scáth's knees and picked her up to ride on his back. It even elicited a laugh from Ven, who was beginning to realize just how special the wolf was. Soon after the party started their way along the edge of the Great Road, Scáth swapped her comfortable spot on the massive back of the wolf with Athvar. And it didn't take long from there for Athvar to start massaging the wolf's shoulders and neck. Faenla's ears dropped backed, and his eyes tightened from the massage. From what Ven and Scáth could decipher, Athvar was even quietly singing an old gnomish hymn into the furry ear.

"Did you use a name when saying goodbye to the wolf?" Ven couldn't help but curl one side of his lips.

Scáth smiled with a slight blush. "I believe I called him Faenla."

Ven immediately raised an eyebrow. "You speak Old Elvish?"

"A little."

Athvar took the opportunity to butt in.

"What's Faenla, meaning?"

Ven began to explain but was enthusiastically outspoken by Scáth.

"Life-long ally." The wolf looked up to Scáth, meeting his crystal blue gaze with her bloomy grey eyes. He gave a knowing squint. Faenla lazily bumped sideways into Scáth and gently licked her cheek.

"He's a friendly one, isn't he!" Athvar chuckled, still comfortably resting on the furry back. Ven admired how perfect a size ratio the gnome and wolf made, much like the taller humanoids were to their steeds.

When the sun had faded and all light was lost to the stars and moons, the party fell to make camp. They agreed on what could be considered the top of a hill in a range that, from their perspective, slightly resembled a wavy ocean of rolling grass. The trio was extra thankful for who they were officially calling Faenla when a fire couldn't be lit, but the wolf could provide ample body heat against a thick coat of fur.

Ven was up long before everyone else as usual. With so frequent of late, he woke up from the same lingering night terror. His body convulsed, and his eyes shot wide as a heavy sweat had consumed him. This time, to his surprise, he noticed the wolf was staring his way. They held each other's gaze for several soothing moments. Ven thought it was as if the wolf understood what he was dreaming. Like it was a story Faenla was familiar with. The wolf broke the gaze by slowly surveying the moonlit horizon. Ven saw the glint in his eye from the minimal light the wolf could use to his advantage. It was much like how the Kyst saw in the dark, simply the evolution of apex predators. The wolf and the Kyst both looked to the southeast when they heard the lone howl of a wolf. Startled, they looked back at each other wide-eyed, and the wolf gave a low whine.

"Go," Ven heard himself confidently say.

Faenla slowly stood up so as not to wake the others and then sprinted off into the distance. It had been nearly five minutes at this point, and Ven had heard no more howls. He thought he could hear footsteps, but being barraged by the constant brushing of tall grass in the wind was disorienting for the coastal elf. It only maddened him when everywhere he sent his vision, he saw no sign of enemies.

"Athvar." Ven shoved the gnome but realized he was far too forceful as Athvar rolled away but was firmly awoken. Then Ven went and gently rocked Scáth awake.

"Ready yourselves," he whispered. Scáth's eyes flashed when she was awoken with the immediate threat of danger.

"Where's Faenla?" she whispered. Athvar was next to them again, mace at the ready.

"Scouting."

Athvar gave a yawn, which betrayed his sense of concern.

The wolf ran for five minutes before digging his claws into the dirt, halting at the smell of a new scent. Another great and extended howl was heard, and this time, Faenla knew it to be close. He darted up and around the centre of a large bluff. He deftly dropped low as a club swung past, poised for his head. The wolf made three more quick darting jumps to face his foe and bit at the arm of the Kintar raider wielding the club. Faenla sunk his fangs in and yanked with such strength it tore the forearm clean off the Kintar's elbow. The raider gave a great roar of pain that echoed out for kilometres. The wolf leaped up and snapped his powerful jaw across the Kintar's throat. With a single clench, the raider's neck broke. Faenla dropped the carcass and sniffed at the strange object the Kintar had strapped to him. Although Faenla was unaware, it was a horn made by goblins to mimic the howl of a wolf.

"Do you hear that?" Scáth asked quietly. Ven had closed his eyes, falling back into the other senses he had been trained to refine and trust. Straining his ears, he knew it to be sure, a Kintar roar in the distance and enemies surrounding them. Athvar was standing much lower, where he could not look over the grass but rather through it. Gnomes had excellent eyes for the dark as they were a burrowing people. Athvar followed an unusual disturbance in the grass until it became evident he was watching a wicked-looking goblin. It didn't stand much taller than Athvar but was battle-scarred, with gnarly piercings across his sickly green skin. He clearly saw the sharply filed teeth and fingernails. This goblin was ready with a blood rusted dagger in each hand. Athvar put a flute to his mouth, he gave a deep exhalation, and a dart struck the neck of the goblin. It made little sound as it fell to the grass, unconscious. In a blindingly quick response, a dagger flew past Athvar's ear, cutting a small gash as it went.

"Goblins, I tell ya!" the gnome shrieked.

The ears of Faenla shot up at the distant sound of Athvar's shriek floating in the wind. He sprang with fury back to his new pack.

Ven threw his right foot back, shifting his stance to the side as a rusty dagger twirled by his neck. Seeing where the goblin had just popped above the grass to throw it, Ven swiftly drew his bow and loosed an arrow into the heart of the goblin. As it fell back, half a dozen more of the pesky goblins popped up out of the grass, throwing daggers and hatchets.

Scáth crouched low and began to focus on not being seen. Soon she began to lose sight of herself for brief periods of time. Occasionally the odd unsuspecting goblin would pass near to her. A Scorn would never let such an opportunity pass by unpunished and made quick work of cutting them down. Ven was now dancing around the many thrown weapons as he quickly became the only visible target. He did, however, manage to line up his many rolls, dives, and twists with one or two goblins to strike with an arrow.

Athvar soon had a pile of no less than seven sleeping goblins when he heard the bone-chilling sound of a Kintar roar. His brew was potent, but sometimes the more stubborn and burly Kintar took several of the laced darts. It wasn't long before a choir of the Kintar battle cries could be heard. Ven knew that they were taunting them. They would often stay hidden, roaring all the while, instilling fear and dread into their enemy. Often, even making their numbers seem greater than what they actually were. A stream of arrows began pelting the dirt around the Kyst. He saw a group of Kintar archers giving support to the approaching raiders. Ven quickly picked up a dead goblin in each hand and hid behind the carcasses. Several arrows made squelching sounds as they thudded into the goblin bodies. One arrow went clean through, skipping off Ven's leather pauldron. By then, the raiders were just a few paces away, and Ven sprang forward, hurling a dead goblin onto the leading attacker. The hunter drew his short-short and used his trident to block the longsword of the next Kintar. Another raider came in swinging a war hammer, aimed for the hunter's head. Ven ducked and used his agility to kick off the first Kintar and slip between the legs of the other. He slashed the brute's ankles as he slipped by. His foe fell, and Ven dragged his trident up his back before triumphantly standing above his fallen enemy.

The Kyst was truly magnificent on that hilltop. He was fully swarmed by an entire band of Kintar but was effortlessly fighting them off with the skill and grace of a legendary warrior. Ven told himself to keep moving and to act on every window of opportunity, keeping his enemies off balance and in each other's way.

Scáth was still hiding in the grass off to the side when an archer who had strayed a little too close to the fray caught her eye. She moved unnoticed and without a sound before coming up behind the archer.

"Guess you didn't see me," Scáth whispered in his ear while plunging the scimitar through his spine. The elven raider fell limply from her sword, and she continued to play the game as best she could. Albeit she was terrified, witnessing the courage and skill of her companions was infectious.

Athvar was flanked by three Kintar raiders slowly surrounding him.

"Uhm, help!" Little did Athvar know, Scáth and Ven were caught in equally perilous situations.

"Tiny gnome, makes for good kicking," one of the Kintar muttered with unparalleled stupidity.

"What! No one will be kicking this gnome!" Athvar declared defiantly and quickly blew two poisoned darts at the brute. The Kintar began choking and grasping at his throat as foam and vile poured between his lips.

"Who's next?" Athvar proudly stated but was immediately interrupted by a large boot. The gnome soared past Scáth, who was struggling to dodge and parry two Kintar who had spotted her sneakily killing. She was holding her own until they entered a flanking position. One raider punched her squarely in the temple, and she hit the ground hard. Ven caught it from the corner of his eye and threw his trident into the head of the Kintar who had struck her. He sacrificed a hit to the back of his head from the butt end of a great axe. He, too, hit the ground hard, dark spots clouding his vision. The hunter turned hot with rage and let out a truly menacing battle cry before coming back up in a tornado of strikes.

The dead Kintar with a trident protruding from its skull fell on top of Scáth, jolting her back to reality. The other raider pulled the dead body off the girl and kicked the scimitar from her hand. Scáth scurried backwards, crawling and kicking to get away from the murderer, when she heard a sound from above. It was a sound that had grown to comfort her during the short time on the coast. From the sky, the SeaRaven that had been following Ven was now dive-bombing the Kintar attacking her. The ShadowScorn couldn't believe her eyes and wasted zero time in retrieving her scimitar. The SeaRaven managed to gouge out an eye before retreating above, and Scáth met the panicked Kintar with a scimitar through the heart

The two raiders that were after Athvar were closing in on him again. The gnome got to one knee, unsure of how to approach this situation. He instinctively crouched as a soaring Faenla bounded over him and landed on both Kintar. The wolf raked his wide and strong paws across the body of one Kintar while maliciously biting the neck of the other.

"Faenla!" Athvar yelled excitedly. Shortly thereafter, one of the many Kintars attempting to fight Ven saw the return of the great wolf and blew a horn signalling their immediate retreat. The party took their fair share of swings and strikes on the retreating enemies, felling several more of the creatures. After a ten-minute skirmish, the hills settled back into an eerie wind.

The wolf sauntered over to Ven, having just ripped his trident from the base of a skull. The Kyst was fuming by himself as if looking for something else to kill, his adrenalin cranked. The wolf nudged Ven's shoulder with his head. The elf looked beside him as if surprised by the presence of Faenla. He dropped his head and shook it slightly, disappointed in himself. Faenla gave him another nudge before fully walking into Ven, pushing the much smaller Kyst back in a playful manner. Ven smiled and sheathed his weapons before crouching low, staring at Faenla. The wolf lowered its head, and Ven sprang at him. Faenla gave way to Ven's weight, falling on his back. Faenla pawed and lightly nipped at the hunter. All the while Ven was being just as playful back, enjoying the tousle with his new companion.

"We probably shouldn't stay here, right?" Scáth asked somewhat rhetorically. Ven and Faenla looked up to her in unison before quickly standing, slightly bashful. They gathered what little they had unpacked and continued on through the darkness of the night.

Not an hour later, they came over a ridge with an excellent view of the Great Road. Ven spotted swaying lanterns hanging off a small caravan of three stagecoaches heading west. The party stopped to look at what they could of the road that connected all sides of Litore. It was a compact stretch of raised land, nearly seven metres across. As the stagecoach made its way, the adventurers spotted the igniting of nearly twenty torches in the surrounding area. A bandit group of highway robbers rode horseback, twenty strong with bandannas covering their faces. Wielding great weapons, and with the element of surprise, the robbers quickly killed off the hired guard. One robber fired a hand crossbow into the heart of the driver. Another reared his horse next to the cart and threw a small ball under it.

From the ridge a small distance off, the party saw a flash of light and the largest stagecoach flip onto its side. No one said anything until the scream of a woman echoed across the valley

"We have to do something!" Scáth unknowingly took a step forward, insisting they take action. Faenla bared his teeth and growled in the direction of the distressed.

"No," Athvar answered solemnly but with a firm tone.

"What do you mean, no?" Scáth turned to face them aggressively.

Ven seemed torn by both sides. It was no doubt the stagecoach was in need of aid, but they were vastly outnumbered. And who was to say the people in the carriage deserved their help. Although, Ven quickly shook that idea out of his head.

"This is the openess of Litore, Scáth. If we stopped at every sign of distress, we wouldn't make it halfway through our journey," Athvar explained.

"I'm well aware of the world we exist in," she shot back to the gnome. "Ven?" She turned her menacing glance at the Kyst. He was more or less at a loss for words. He knew going down there was the right thing to do. He also knew it would more than likely mean their ultimate demise.

"Athvar has travelled these roads before. Are times like these not why we wanted him here?"

She couldn't believe the words coming from someone that should understand. Not a month ago, it was Scáth in that carriage defenceless, and before that, it was her abduction in her own bedroom safely tucked away in ShadowScorn Castle.

"Fine," she said with disdain.

The party broke an hour later to sleep away what few hours of the night remained. As Ven meditated deeply and Athvar lay fast asleep, Scáth quietly got up and walked out of the camp. Faenla, always somewhat on guard, noticed this and slowly got up to join her. Much like before, the wolf picked up Scáth between her knees and sprang back in the direction of the stagecoach.

CHAPTER TEN
The Right Thing

Scáth sat on the back of Faenla, leaning forward, arms wrapped securely around his neck.

"Thank you."

The pair sprinted through the night and made it back to the crashed stagecoach in less than twenty minutes. Scáth got off to survey the crash while Faenla went to discern which direction the bandits fled. The Scorn nimbly climbed on top of the overturned stagecoach where the door, which was now attached only by one hinge, lay ajar. She jumped down inside feet first. The moonlight shone through the opened door to reveal the interior with a pale light. She found little but broken glass and splintered wood, except for a plush doll of an elven noble dressed in a fanciful gown. The realization abruptly hit her. Scáth grabbed the doll and jumped out of the carriage. She landed next to an awaiting Faenla and quickly climbed on his back.

Faenla sprang down the trail. He briskly padded for some fifteen minutes before they both could hear the drunken celebrations of humans. They came over a hill and noticed a camp on the edge of a swampy pond. A great bonfire illuminated the revelry, surrounded by canvas tents, glowing and dancing in the firelight.

"Stay here and listen for me; I may need you," Scáth whispered in Faenla's ear. He gave a knowing squint and perched low atop the hill, vigilantly watching his prey. Scáth donned her hood and focused on being one with the shadow around her. She prowled her way closer until hiding in a small thicket of bushes next to one tent. From there, she could hear most conversations with a degree of clarity.

A finely dressed man, wearing a decorated hat with an exotic feather protruding one side and a silver rapier strapped to his hip, emerged from the largest tent.

"Did you secure her?" he addressed a more mangey-looking human with matted black curls and shaggy facial hair.

"Yes, sir, far tent, she's got nowhere to go," he answered with delighted macabre.

"Good. Join the others." He dismissed his gang member and walked toward the tent that held the prisoner. Scáth manoeuvred around most of the camp, using bushes, tents, and the odd crate to hide behind while following the leader. She halted as two robbers came around a corner in a drunken stupor and began to urinate on her boots. She dare not breathe, if not out of fright then for the sick smell. With bladders emptied, the two drunks moved to refill their tankards, none the wiser. She scurried on, just in time to catch the leader walking through the flaps of the prisoner's tent.

Ven and Athvar had awoken to a shiver, with their main heat source gone.

"What do you suppose we do?" asked Ven. Athvar was genuinely surprised, but the Kyst felt silly for not predicting this.

"At least the wolf went with her," Athvar added with brevity. Ven swept the long hair back from his eyes and looked out into the open vastness with genuine humility.

"What are we doing out here? We've barely begun, and very little has gone our way. Perhaps we should turn around before it's too late," Ven said, beaten.

"Why would ya of all folk turn around now, if not just to spite yourself, eh? It's no secret among those who know ya. The orphan Kyst, Guardian of the North, yearning for a life such as this," Athvar offered retrospectively.

Ven looked out into the night. "Maybe I know not what I want."

Scáth made it to the other side of the camp and even into the tent unnoticed. Inside was pitch black, except for a lit candelabra held by the leader. A small Solsta elven girl, no more than ten years of age, sat tied to the main pole of the tent. Of course, the inferior eyes of humans limited him to the sight of his candlelight, but the ShadowScorn could see everything in the room with detail.

"My apologies for the roughness of my men. Their manners are few and dusty."

Scáth could clearly see the girl had been grabbed roughly a few times.

"What do you want?" she asked vehemently. The leader laughed at the fiery spirit this little elf seemed possessed of.

"Just the coin you are worth, my dear." Scáth drew her scimitar from its sheathe while he was speaking and slowly crept forward, inherently never making a sound.

"If you make no trouble, I assure you everything will be fine."

At this point, the elven girl, also with superior vision, noticed a stalking form behind her captor. "Who are you going to sell me to?" she asked.

"Well, it depends..." He was interrupted by a scimitar appearing through his chest, Scáth whispered in his ear and covered his mouth with her free hand.

"We have a saying in ShadowScorn. In the end, darkness takes us all."

She could feel the steam release from his mouth and escape between her fingers as the scimitar stole the air from his lungs. She held his mouth tight until he fell completely still, then she slowly lowered his body to the ground. The elven girl cowered in fear but made no sign of making noise.

"I'm here to free you," Scáth whispered while untying the rope. As soon as the girl was free, she ran to the other side of the tent, terrified.

Scáth, unsure what to do next, pulled out the doll and offered it to the child.

"I promise, I only wish to see you returned to your family," she whispered warmly.

"Promise?" the little girl asked.

"Promise."

The child nodded and grasped Scáth's hand tightly. She tore the cloak off the leader and draped it around the elf. Peeking out the front, she saw the majority of the bandits were now drinking and celebrating in full merriment. They made their exit quickly and without a hitch.

Walking up the hill, Scáth thought it best to give the child a fair warning of Faenla.

"I have someone I want you to meet. I think you are going to like him." Scáth was trying to elicit some excitement out of the girl.

"Him?" was all that the little one could muster, which made Scáth's heart sink. Just then, the pair stopped in their tracks as Faenla, shot his pointy ears up out of the grass. Scáth saw a smile cross the child's face. Soon, Faenla was upon them and Scáth felt the girl squeeze her hand all the tighter as the wolf stood a solid metre above her.

"Whoa," she said in amazement. Faenla looked down on the girl and gave her a long loving lick across her face. The child belly laughed, and Faenla dropped his front legs, inviting them onto his back.

Soon the trio were sprinting back toward Ven and Athvar.

"Perhaps," Athvar answered, slightly defeated by Ven's stubbornness. The pair turned to the sound of a familiar howl. In the distance, they spotted Faenla cresting a hill with two on his back.

"Looks like Lady Scáth was successful," Athvar proudly exclaimed, as if never doubting it for a minute. The hunter wore an expression of delight and relief. Faenla reared up next to the Kyst and gnome. Scáth got off and helped the elven girl down. Athvar gave Faenla some dried meat for a job well done. Ven walked over to the pair and got down on one knee to meet the girl's height. He pulled back his hood, revealing those opalescent green eyes and thick swept-back hair.

"Hello, my name is Ven." He even dipped his torso in a little bow to the girl. She leaned against Scáth nonchalantly.

"My name is Hera," she spoke slightly aloof, and understandably enough, Ven thought.

"It's good to meet you, Hera." He stood up, looking to Scáth. She was clearly disappointed with her companions, save Faenla, of course.

"I expect better from you and Athvar. If we're going to—" Scáth was interrupted by Ven, who put his hands on her shoulders and said genuinely.

"—We were wrong." Ven hugged Scáth tightly. "Thank you for

showing me that." He was happy that Scáth had done what she thought was right. It served as a good reminder of what he was doing out here in the first place. Scáth hugged him back, both truly happy at that moment. Athvar had introduced himself and was petting a lounging Faenla with the child.

"Where are you from?" the plucky gnome asked while scratching the wolf's giant ear.

"Erindore. Can you take me there, maybe, please?" she asked politely and hopefully.

"I think we could do that! Don't you, Faenla?" Athvar asked the wolf. He gave a squint and nuzzled Hera with his large snout. She giggled and snuggled up against Faenla, rubbing her face in his thick, warm fur.

Ven looked to Scáth. "It would appear we're making a stop to Erindore."

"I think Faenla and I will wait outside of town while the three of you go in." Scáth's reasoning became clear quickly to Ven, and so it was settled. They were only a day and a half from the large trading settlement of Erindore. With the sun's light beginning to fill the eastern horizon, the party decided to start their day now.

They thought it best to stay further away from the road in case any more bandit patrols were out looking for the missing bounty. The next short leg of their journey was undisturbed. Highwaymen and monsters didn't normally roam so close to larger settlements. The acting local authority often hired adventures to clear the land up to a certain distance around the communities. Upon spotting the walls and gates of Erindore, a city of nearly ten thousand, Ven found himself overwhelmed by the density of population. Mostly humans and elves but some dwarves and halflings roamed the bustling streets. Scáth and Faenla stayed a good distance back, finding their own sun-swept field to relax in and cook a meal now they were safely out of the wilds.

Ven, Athvar, and Hera walked through the gates. Upon passing two guards, the Kyst immediately noted both of them giving him a strange look. With nothing more than glances exchanged, he kept moving and let it serve as a reminder to be on his guard, perhaps even more than usual here. The town was poor in most accounts. Peasant farmers made up the majority of the population, while an active trade market made up most of the business and excitement. Winter's frost and snow had at least solidified the otherwise soggy ground it was built on.

"Do you know where to go?" Athvar asked Hera. She nodded enthusiastically and yanked on his arm to follow.

A few restful hours later, Scáth was seated next to a small fire when she spotted Ven and Athvar approaching. She noted early only Ven had a satchel with a single strap across his torso.

"Hera made it home?" Scáth inquired with great importance.

"She walked us right up to her front door," Athvar said happily. The gnome seemed more thrilled than usual when Scáth noticed much of his face was covered in powdered sugar. She then had to react quickly as Ven tossed a hefty sack of coins at her.

"Turns out Hera's father is brother to the Duke of Erindore. Before you ask, he insisted we take the compensation," Ven said with a wide grin.

"Bought us a whole ton of sweets and supplies, Lady Scáth," Athvar added, backing up Ven's claim.

"Nothing wrong with enjoying the spoils of a good deed," Scáth said excitedly, looking inside the satchel before shoving a flaky and fluffy pastry in her mouth.

"Onwards," she said with a mouthful of deliciousness. They took advantage of the last hour or so left of the light.

After a few kilometres had passed, the group came to what looked like a dried-out marsh between two large hills. Seated neatly on stilts in the middle of it all was an abandoned hunting cabin.

"That looks promising." Scáth began walking closer to the cabin after surveying it for a moment.

"Wait," Athvar protested. He looked to Faenla, they stared at each other, and soon, the wolf was off to check the cabin.

"Best we let him sniff it out first," Athvar's obvious point being that animals were far more attuned to the presence of other creatures than humanoids often were. Faenla climbed up the rickety stairs and pawed the door open. Nothing more than a few rats scurried out from the floorboards. They spent the night out of the cold wind and frozen ground. There was even a few dried logs left next to the small stove.

CHAPTER ELEVEN
A World Away

High in a tower on the sunny coast of Serenstrom sat a council of five dignitaries in the Holy Temple of Sesara. The entire massive cathedral glistened in the sun from a white mortar filled with pearls and a paint made from powdered seashells. Dozens of more turrets protruding far into the sky sparkled like beacons of hope and light. It sat high in the very centre of Serenstrom, a man-made island off the coast of Litore. From the temple cascaded thousands upon thousands of equally iridescent homes and buildings of various shapes and sizes that eventually verged on the Boundless Ocean.

The leading members of the church sat around a grand marble table. Carved across its surface was their benevolent Goddess, Sesara, performing many of her fabled miracles. One human man sat at the head of the table on a raised ornate chair. His hair was white with age, and the wrinkles of time carved deeply across his skin. He was adorned in long silver and gold robes. Bedecked in many necklaces and rings that were all possessed of great magical abilities and spells. None more magnificent than the shimmering crown that slightly levitated above his fine hair.

"Why have we not heard from those who were leading the Sanctuary Island operation?" His powerful voice echoed off the marbled walls.

A much younger human male, who was of high repute in his order but clearly hesitant to deliver their leader the bad news, shifted awkwardly.

"When Paladin Ilzar had not sent word, one of our wizards teleported himself with a small security force to the island." The younger man named Berek choked on his words for a moment. "They found the original team, slaughtered, Your Benevolence," Berek finished with his head held low in shame. The Macer and leader of the religious zealots, O'Donnell, held a heavy and unimpressed stare upon him.

"How?" he snapped back; the crown slightly pulsed with his anger.

"We are unsure." Berek's voice cracked. A human woman known as Aunna Morningthorne sat across from Berek. She was in her early thirties, with long raven-coloured hair that swept past her waist, vividly complimenting her eyes of a similar hue. A simple golden headband with a ruby, encrusted front and centre, encircled her forehead. She was a cleric for her order and had spent many of her years researching the extensive cultures of Litore.

"I believe it was a singular Kyst However, my colleagues continue to rebuff that opinion." She was confident in her speech, unlike Berek.

"It would appear the ShadowScorn has found a protector in a local Kyst elf. Yet, many of us doubt three of our greatest warriors could be slain by a single combatant," Berek implied, which received a menacing glance from Aunna.

"What would you know of elves?" her words dripped with disrespect.

"How is our ally?" Macer asked with impatience, and before Berek could respond, a heavier set man with an unfortunate number of boils on his nose spoke up.

"As we know, Uthul made a great commander in the destruction of Silva. He even took it upon himself to capture the Prince of Silva in an effort to set him loose on the Kyst travelling with the girl," the heavier man, known as the 'Igon of Serenstrom', stated gleefully. He was in charge of the many churches and temples of Sesara across Litore and made a point of finding interesting people along his travels. Uthul 'The Betrayer' being one of them.

"Will Uthul partake in the coming attack?" Macer asked devilishly, clearly enthused by the news. The other members looked around at one another. It was clear that Igon and the Macer were in on something everyone else was not. Ivan, the last member of the council, was known simply as Ivan 'The Revered', a Paladin of their faith. He intertwined his fingers which supported his chin while sharing a curious look with Aunna. Ivan had shocks of grey thrown into his deep brown hair and a thick but neatly maintained beard. He was similar to the Macer in experience and standing but was all too aware of what power does to men and women. Ivan had sat on many courts across Litore as a servant to the varied kings and queens, acting as a guide in the name of Sesara. That experience had gifted him the ability to separate himself from the mind sickness that was associated with power.

"He showed great enthusiasm, Your Benevolence." Igon was clearly rubbing the ego of the Macer.

"Why was I unaware there was to be another campaign?" Ivan was the general of all paladins in their faith and normally the first to know about war efforts. The council wasn't sure, but it seemed as though Ivan was accusing their leader. Macer stared at Ivan, choosing the right words to put him in his place, but Igon interrupted.

"We were going to make it known soon, I assure you, Ivan."

"Are you the Macer?" Ivan was flat in his response, speaking to Igon as if he were a child. Igon sat there awkwardly and allowed their leader to speak.

"We here are under the impression, as directly expressed by our Goddess, that the ShadowScorn are a mockery to life and all Sesara stands for. Correct?" Igon, Aunna, and Berek nodded in unison and whispered a short prayer to their deity. Ivan remained steadfast.

"No," Ivan answered defiantly. "A message misinterpreted many centuries ago. The ShadowScorn are peaceful and continue to remain so." Ivan was well aware that the capture and selling of ShadowScorn had become exponentially more frequent with the rise of Macer O'Donnell.

"Wrong!" yelled the Macer. "Aceia, the God of Shadow, spat in the very face of Sesara when he created the Scorn. It is our faithful duty to rid these creatures of her presence."

"Then what is your plan, Your Benevolence?" Ivan retorted with feigned agreement. His heart sank when all he saw was the corner of the Macer's mouth rise in an evil smirk.

He woke up groggy, one eye swollen shut from the merciless beatings he had suffered the days prior. The sound of arguing Kintar was muffled as the Kyst noticed his left eardrum was burst, covering his jaw and neck in crusty blood. Shivering, the hunter pulled his legs close to his chest, dragging his lower half across the cold, wet, cobblestone floor of his prison cell. The sound of chain links scraping the ground gnawed at him as he shifted his legs. He wasn't sure how long the arguing had been going on, but it was too muffled for him to understand. He slowly pushed his back against the wall and slid along it so he was sitting upright. The pain from the multitude of deep cuts and large bruises made him want to vomit while doing so, but he could tell the arguing had abruptly ceased. With the back of his head against the wall in support of staying vertical, the Prince of Silva stared at the iron door of his cell, waiting.

He figured it was most likely that the Kintar would just kill him in any one of the innumerable and horrible ways they knew how. He couldn't believe he was still alive and wasn't sure if that was even what he wanted. After a tense few moments and only a couple more murmurs heard, the door flew inwards to slam against the wall. Much to his surprise, a fellow Kyst walked in. He could barely see through his one open eye, for it was very bloodshot. Yet, it was obvious to the prince that this was Uthul 'The Betrayer.' The murderer of his mother, how unfortunate it was, Rexous did not know that.

"It does my heart well to see you alive." Uthul knelt in front of the chained-up prince.

"It must do your heart equally well to see me chained so. I know you hated my mother, but unfortunately for you, there is no Silva left to rule." Rexous cared little for the gentleness Uthul offered.

"On the contrary, My Prince. Your mother was the closest thing I knew to true love. The Kintar I find myself aligned with now and again would never have been near Silva if it were not for the 'Mighty Ven Devar' harbouring the ShadowScorn." Uthul was trying harder than usual. He had big plans that could succeed if the persuasion of this powerful ally was done right.

Rex, as badly beaten and bruised as he was, strategically bit back from saying something he could use as leverage later. "What do you want from me?" the young Kyst said indignantly. "I am the prince of nothing. Silva is gone."

"I saved you because she would have wanted you to survive. Now you must pay us back by avenging your mother." Uthul was clearly offering something.

"By killing every last Kintar in the Northern Rainforest?" Rex replied sarcastically.

"No," Uthul spoke gravely. "By hunting down Ven Devar and bringing an end to the destruction he sows."

Rexous couldn't necessarily disagree with the logic, although he didn't understand what Uthul had to gain or why he was in the position to offer him this stay of death. He had always hated Ven Devar, of that he knew. At least he considered it to be hate. Their rivalry dated back to when they were mere children. They were close in age and of nearly equal skill, both known among their people as the greatest warrior Kyst in the north. However, the Prince of Silva was constantly outperformed by Ven Devar on hunts, which sparked even greater disdain for the orphan.

"He travels along the Great Road as we speak. My scouts have confirmed it," Uthul added slyly. Rexous sat there leaning against the wall of his cell. He had an undeniable urge pushing him for the revenge of his mother. "We believe he's heading to ShadowSc—"

"—Enough!" Uthul was interrupted by an irate Rexous. "You have said all I care to hear, Uthul 'The Betrayer.' Leave me to my thoughts and await your answer. And bring me a damn blanket."

Uthul nodded and stood upright, exiting the cell. His chest heaving with animosity, Rexous began breathing long and deep, centring himself. Everything the Kyst had prepared for his entire life was stolen that fiery night. And he had barely been conscious enough since it happened to work through the traumatic experience.

On Sanctuary Island, Vakar was walking around the trunks of great trees collecting different fungi and berries into a wooden bowl. After gathering what he needed, the sage walked through the wet snow to a camp he had set up for himself. It consisted of a large tent, a warm ever-burning fire, and other basic amenities.

He went over to a table that held many tools of alchemy and books sprawled across its surface. Vakar loved working outside. Before, that used to mean working outside in the tree canopy. Not here, though. No predators meant he could work in peace, completely undisturbed on the soul-soothing forest floor.

Vakar put his collected items into a mortar and pestle and began turning them into a paste. From there, he added an almost acidic liquid that made the substance briefly boil. What was leftover from the boil was then mixed in with saltwater. He dropped a singular iridescent strand of silver hair from between his fingertips that floated down and rested atop the water. He mixed the hair into the liquid with a glass stir stick before adding a virosa cap into the now purple liquid. Soon, the mushroom cap had absorbed two-thirds of the liquid, and Vakar poured the remaining substance delicately into a glass vial and sealed it with wax. Once sealed, the liquids formed a vaporous layer on the bottom few millimetres. Vakar held it close to his eyes and frowned at his perfect poison as he watched the now almost completely translucent liquid swirl atop the silver vapours.

He began back toward the village of Hearth. It was dark by the time Vakar had arrived, and a wet snow had started to fall. He met with Queen Ilthanis and the now temporary ruler of Silva's people in the town square. The pair strode off to her private bungalow as they had done so often of late. Soon they were seated and enjoying dinner, overlooking the Northern Archipelago.

"How do the sages fair in the rebuilding?" Ilthanis was optimistic that Vakar would make Silva magnificent again.

"Excellent. The trees have been planted, over the next month we begin the ritual process of exponentially aging them for rebuilding," he offered with happiness in his heart. However, Ilthanis could sense something was off about him tonight. To Vakar's credit, he was acting normal, but the several hundred years of life she had lived told her there was something distracting him.

"Then your people will soon prosper again," she said kindly, thinking that would put a smile on his face. Vakar could tell the queen saw something was wrong and so he quickly changed the topic.

"Allow me to refill our drinks." He smiled flirtatiously. He knew Ilthanis had been giving him subtle stares and clues of her interest. It flattered him more than excited him. He was in no place to love again for some time, perhaps ever. That didn't mean he wouldn't use Ilthanis' lust for him to his own advantage.

She handed the Kyst her glass, and he left the veranda of the bungalow to refill the drinks inside. Between filling the glasses with wine, he poured just a drop of the liquid from the vial into the queen's glass. Returning to the small terrace, he handed her the drink, resting a hand on her shoulder. They clinked glasses and drank the entirety of their wine in one go. Ilthanis met Vakar's hand with her own, she squeezed tightly, and he pulled her up from the chair. He grabbed her by the waist with his other hand, pulling her close before gently caressing her lips.

CHAPTER TWELVE
Push Through

We near a month since leaving Sanctuary Island, and it has been all have I ever dreamt of and more. I am truly thankful to have the companions I walk beside on this long journey. I know the return trip will not be as tantalizing without Scáth, but I look forward to it nonetheless. That's to say if there will be a return trip. We still have another month of dangerous trekking ahead of us. I fear much can and will happen to us in that time. Yet, in that fear, I find a sense of excitement that draws me nearer to its discovery. As I sit awake in the late hours of my companion's rest, I wonder who or what lingers around the next corner we take. All of it pains me to consider that it will soon come to an end, and I will once again be left in a home and society that will forever seem alien to me. Silva never was a home for me and its people never a family, of that I can confidently say. When I return and the people rebuild their magnificent city, as I know they will, I will be given more responsibility, tradition, and recognition than ever before as King of Silva. How did that happen? It was never my intention to have such power. Why had Vakar distanced himself from me since learning of that fact? Perhaps the loss of Qiri changed the Kyst I once considered my brother. Certainly less had changed greater people, and if that is the truth, then I cannot blame him. I believe everyone who survived that night was changed in some way or another; it truly was the reality of nightmares. I am thankful for all that the Kyst of Silva did for me in my youth. Rescuing me as a baby from a lone floating dingy to housing me and training me to be the hunter I am. For that, I feel a great debt of gratitude and with it, guilt. They rescued me and gave me a life, now I had the chance to lead them and pay them back for all their generosity. Instead, I leave at the first opportunity available and disappear for months on some fool's honour-bound errand. Every time I look at Scáth or hear her melodic voice, I am reminded of and feel the confidence I first had in deciding to see her home safely. If every road was easy, we would never be given the opportunity to grow from our stumbles.

-Ven Devar

As the adventurers, Faenla, and now many prairie critters crested one rolling hill, they were met with a marsh so vast it was all but unavoidable. A heavy, soup-like fog hung in the air as the smell of scum-layered water and rotting debris permeated their nostrils.

"Nope," Athvar exclaimed matter-of-factly.

"Yes," Scáth replied insistently. Faenla went to sniffing the area and gave a low whine.

"If I'm not picked off by some swamp swimming creature, I'll surely drown before ya even have to get yar belly's wet." The gnome was in a defiant mood, and Faenla snorted in a mocking tone while looking at Athvar.

"You don't get a vote!" Athvar yelled at the wolf, which brought a smile to Scáth's face.

"What choice do we have, friend?" Ven asked of Athvar.

"We take the Great Road," the gnome nearly begged.

"It goes through the same marsh, just as dangerous and seemingly easier for those after Scáth to find her." Ven was honestly surprised Athvar was reacting with such a fuss. As the gnome stood staring at the marsh, the group noticed a serious look of defeat cross his little round face.

"I've had bad experiences with such places." With his words being merely a whisper, Faenla walked over to Athvar and lowered his large furry head to lick the gnome across the cheek. Then lowered further, inviting Athvar onto his back.

"Thank you," Athvar said, climbing onto the enormous wolf. Athvar and Faenla took up the rear, keeping a keen eye on what they could around them. Ven was always in search of the most solid and stable ground. The fog made that task immensely more difficult with the limited range of sight. The occasional disturbance on the surface of the water as a creature came swimming in search of food, kept everyone on edge. Ven let his extensive knowledge of environments guide his steps through the all too random and soggy terrain. It was never easy to tell if a body of water, small or large was only a dozen centimetres in-depth or had the bottom of a lake. Whenever the group was forced to cross over a section of water, Ven used his trident in its elongated form to test the ground in front of him.

Nearing the end of the first day, the group made a crossing through a thigh deep body of water. Past the halfway point, Faenla's rear paw sunk into a deep hole, and Athvar tumbled off his back into the murky liquid. The great wolf began to panic when he couldn't tug his paw free of the underwater divot.

"Athvar!" Scáth screamed as she quickly turned around, rushing through the thigh-high water toward him. Ven whipped around when he heard Scáth shouting and saw the disaster unfolding. He instantly felt the anxiety surrounding Faenla. Athvar sank quickly with all his gear and clothes on. His feet touched bottom, and he swam violently as the water was just barely above his head, alas he proved too heavy. He felt a sudden jolt of pain and disorientation as Faenla's other rear paw, kicking all the while to help get free, nailed him square in the chin. Athvar went soaring through the water and could tell he was now sinking deeper. His throat began to quiver spastically for air. He kicked and flapped the best he could to swim toward the surface but the light above only diminished.

Scáth ran past Faenla with furious intent and saw a distorted reflection of Athvar. All Ven saw was Scáth diving into the wider and deeper section of this seeming puddle. He rushed over to the wolf and held his kicking paw steady. Ven shoved his arm as low onto Faenla's stuck ankle as possible and yanked as hard as he could. Faenla gave a yelp of pain as both of them strained with all their strength.

Scáth dived down three-metres before grabbing onto the drowning gnome. It took her little effort to ascend to the surface of the water and onto the tall weeds off to the side. Ven heard a huge suction noise, and a bubble of air burst from the water. He and the wolf went flying onto the grass with a wet thud. Ven quickly hurried over to Scáth and Athvar. He was coughing out brown-coloured water, which quickly turned into him vomiting out anything else he had consumed that day.

"How much more of this, Ven?" Scáth asked with great worry in her voice as she caught her breath.

"At this rate, I guess another three days further to reach the edge. But I don't truthfully know," he replied apologetically. "Perhaps Athvar was right."

Scáth just shook her head and looked back to the now unconscious Athvar, lying wet amongst the weeds. Confident in this fog that a fire would not give them away, Ven went to gather what dry weeds and materials he could. Athvar didn't wake until late into the night. Much to his surprise, he found himself stripped to his undergarments and wrapped tightly in Ven's PumaSheep cloak, tucked between Faenla's shoulder and neck. Athvar was equally surprised by the warmth and coziness he felt and promptly went back to sleep.

Scáth had hung her and Athvar's clothes to dry over the measly fire. She was now in a spare base layer of clothes, wrapped up in her cloak nestled next to Ven, who was actively stoking the fire and adding what little he could to maintain its heat.

"How do you keep going?" Scáth asked plainly while resting her head on Ven's shoulder as she gazed into the fire. He was caught off guard by the question. In his eyes, he simply didn't see any other choice.

"You are the only thing that can prevent your own demise. In the wild, to stop is to die," he answered honestly.

"I know that," she replied softly. "How do you continue to live by your tenets with such devotion?"

Ven thought about it for a moment, leaving the duo in the silence of the fog-ridden bog.

"Perhaps, I only indulge my self-doubts in moments such as these. When we are on the road and surrounded by an ever-changing environment, I must trust that my values have taken me this far. In my heart, I am a hunter first, and that means honour dictates certain things of me. I actively wonder if I was wrong in seeing you home so soon after the destruction of Silva. But when you saved that girl from those bandits, it reminded me that right and wrong should always take precedence in our decisions. I pledged my protection over you that night we met in the woods, and I plan to see you safely reunited with your home."

Scáth wrapped an arm around the hunter's torso, he pulled her close under his arm, and she promptly fell to slumber. Ven looked down to see her in a deep sleep; however, the coastal blue eyes of Faenla caught his attention. They both looked out in the direction of where they would set off tomorrow, even though there was only fog to view.

"What do you think awaits us?" Ven asked the wolf in his native tongue of Kystin. Faenla looked back to Ven and offered an uneasy exhalation.

"I sense it too," Ven softly said with worry. He had never spent time in a marsh, aside from the occasional bog in the lower sunken areas of the rainforest. He was most unfamiliar with the creatures that lay ahead of them in a practical sense. The research and knowledge of Litore's many creatures was an extensive part of the Kyst's training as a hunter or sage.

He found little rest that night. It wasn't uncommon during hunts back in Silva for the Kyst to go several days without sleep. So Ven spent that night mentally and physically preparing himself for his planned 'stay of rest.' The hunter's began a meditation as children that would allow them to override their body's need for rest and healing. Over the centuries, some hunters became so proficient in the meditation they could have a 'stay of rest' for weeks at a time before eventually being forced by their body into a deep sleep.

Ven opened his eyes from meditation when he knew Scáth had finished dressing into her still soggy clothes. The duo heard a muffled voice speak from under a pile of Faenla's fur.

Scáth grabbed the equally dried-out clothes of Athvar and went to shoeing Faenla off the trapped gnome. Faenla was honestly surprised after he got up and noticed a flattened Athvar lying there. Once Scáth and Athvar had eaten and were geared up, they noticed Ven had just finished attaching something to the wolf. The pair walked over to the curious scene.

"How does that feel?" Ven quietly asked Faenla as he was adjusting a few lengths of rope he had tied around the shoulders and belly of the proud wolf. Faenla licked him on the face and gave his re-affirming squint.

"What are you about, Ven?" Scáth voiced with interest. He was too busy putting the final touches on the series of knotted ropes to answer. Athvar walked up to and around Faenla, inspecting the design, when he noticed identical rope loops on either shoulder. He did not think this possible if it were not for Ven's knowledge of nautical rigging.

"Is this what I think it is?" he asked with obvious derisiveness. Ven looked to the gnome with a wry grin.

"If you're thinking it's something between a saddle and a harness, you'd be right!" Ven was proud of his quick fix to Athvar's height problem in the marsh; the idea had come to him in his meditation. Faenla bent his front paws to his knees so Athvar could climb up. Upon reaching the wolf's back, he noticed a thick rope that wrapped around Faenla's large chest. It offered the perfect handle for the gnome to hold on to. Ven slid the make-shift stirrups and looped them over the gnome's feet.

"Wow," escaped Athvar's mouth. Ven smiled with a sense of relief knowing Athvar would feel better about continuing the journey, now safely secured on the back of Faenla.

With that, the party continued their perilous and trying journey through the unforgiving marshes of the Morass Prairie. Athvar found himself thankful for having the rope on more than one occasion when Faenla unexpectedly dipped or jerked while crossing water.

Halfway through the day, a large gust of wind blew through the marsh. The fog opened for a brief moment when Scáth noticed something watching them in the distance. It was a figure similar to her own, but the hair was in thin greasy strands, and her clothes were tattered, hanging to her like clumps. The figure gave a smile, and her yellow rotted teeth spewed swamp water through the cracks. Scáth wanted to call for her companions to notice, but the words simply wouldn't leave her mouth. No matter how hard she struggled, Scáth couldn't break eye line with the monstrosity. She was screaming internally to herself now, hoping, wishing, her friends would help.

"Ven!" Scáth screamed until there was simply no air left in her lungs, her voice trailing off in a coarse roughness. Yet, as the words escaped her mouth and the Kyst did in fact turn to look, the figure was gone, and the fog resettled. Ven rushed to the ShadowScorn's side as she now held her face between her palms, weeping and kneeling in the grass.

He slid through the grass to kneel beside her, holding her tight. "What happened?" When he elicited no response, he looked to Athvar, who wore an equally concerned expression.

"There's someone... someone's out there." The fright was clear in her voice, and as she looked up to the Kyst, a sudden disassociation fell upon her.

"C'mon, milady. We have a purpose, and we mustn't forget it," Ven said the words with such kindness, but they seemingly bounced off the ShadowScorn. Scáth remained emotionally unresponsive for the rest of their trek that day.

The party broke earlier than usual as the fog had a tendency to drown out the day's light sooner than that of a clear open field. Scáth was still displaying a level of scatteredness that concerned both Ven and Athvar. The gnome had told Scáth, that Faenla was shedding, and all the loose hair was choking him every time a breeze kicked up. Faenla gave an incredulous look to Athvar, clearly unimpressed with the idea of being groomed. Scáth didn't have an opinion and took the brush from Athvar. She and Faenla laid down near the weak fire while they talked quietly away from camp.

"What happened to her?" Ven whispered to Athvar while keeping an eye on them.

"I saw nothing. Faenla and I were forced to stop when she did. Neither of us saw anything, Ven." The gnome shook his head doubtfully. It was agreed that Athvar and Faenla were actively looking out for threats while Ven and Scáth found the best route through the marsh. So how could they have missed it?

"I can barely get her to speak."

"Perhaps, we walk through the night?" Athvar posited quite optimistically. Ven didn't hate that idea, everyone saw in the dark with relative ease. He admired the gnome for his courage after the incident that almost saw him at the bottom of a deep, dark bog. Either way, Ven figured the sooner they were out, the sooner they could get Scáth help.

"Yes, we walk the night. With an even pace, we'll make the other side by tomorrow eve." Before Athvar could even share his delight at the Kyst's decision, they both heard the melodic voice of Scáth. She was still brushing Faenla and began singing a nursery rhyme in Old Elvish. The hunter and gatherer looked on in confusion. Faenla was sitting on all fours as Scáth was singing, the wolf looking to Ven with uncertainty. All three of them shot their gaze out past the singing

Scáth to a single drawn-out scream of a man in terror. Ven drew his trident and scanned the horizon. Athvar's eyes looked like they were about to pop out of his head. Faenla tried standing up, but the still singing Scáth gripped a handful of fur in one fist. The wolf gave a great yelp and sat back down, unsure of what to do. Another scream from the same man echoed through the dark moonlite marsh. The sound of a single sword parry skipped across the air.

"Check on Scáth. Do not move after that, Athvar. Do you understand me?" Ven snapped sternly.

"I understand," he replied with a shaky voice. The hunter darted off in the direction of the distressed, pacing and counting his steps as he went. A minute later, the hunter heard the sound of clashing steel once more. Straining to do so, he spotted a large humanoid with semi-pointed ears and small tusks, fending off a pack of bandits with his double-bearded battle-axe. Ven threw a dagger into a bandit sneaking behind the large man. That caused the figure to turn and lose focus; he subsequently got hit in the temple and fell hard to the ground. Ven managed to drop three of the bandits on his way over. The closer the hunter got, the more obvious it became that these weren't bandits but average travellers.

Athvar approached Scáth and Faenla slowly. She was still singing that song, and Athvar found it to be far more haunting than soothing.

"Lady Scáth?" He walked a little bit closer. Faenla tried to stand up again but felt Scáth's grip tighten again before he fully attempted it.

"Lady Scáth?" he said again with growing fear. She slowly turned her head and stopped singing. She made eye contact with the gnome just as the skin-crawling cackle of a Bog Witch filled the air. The ShadowScorn's eyes looked hollowed-out with darkness as writhing shadow clung to her brow and cheekbone.

"Let go of Faenla." He drew his mace while indignantly insisting Scáth let go of the wolf. Athvar knew Faenla could break away anytime he wanted but was most likely afraid of hurting the Scorn. Athvar gripped the head of the mace and held the wooden handle out.

"Ah ha haha hahaha." Scáth broke out in hysterical laughter as she began matching the cackles of the Bog Witch. Athvar smacked Scáth's hand free of Faenla's fur, who immediately darted up and nimbly pounced on the woman. Pinning her to the ground with all four mighty paws, Faenla gave her a big lick. Athvar quickly went to fill his ears with ground-up tobacco. He could already feel his sanity slipping from the unrelenting and horrifying laugh penetrating his mind. While Scáth was pinned to the ground, Athvar filled her ears as well.

"Keep watch for the witch, Faenla," the gnome yelled while frantically looking through his many satchels.

Ven reached the sight of the unconscious man. Upon briefly getting a better look, the Kyst assumed he was of mixed orcish and elven heritage. The mixed-blood was a hulking figure with a green to red gradient skin tone. Ven ducked as a small wooden chest went flying over his head. He looked to see a finely dressed and plump man running toward him, fists flailing. Ven took pity and spun the pommel of his trident into the temple of the man. The human male hit the ground hard and fast. It was clear now that the witch was stealing the minds of travellers on the Great Road for her own use. The hunter heard the laughs of the Bog Witch and took heart knowing she had no power over his mind. For the elves of Litore were impervious to magic dealing with the mind and soul.

Ven was almost tackled by two travellers under the witch's spell as they simultaneously jumped at his front and back. He quick-stepped to one side, letting the two knock heads, and fall relatively unharmed to the ground. He heard the cackling witch growing nearer and many approaching footsteps. Kneeling beside the half-orc with haste, Ven simply slapped him across the face as hard as he could. The brute sprang his back up and grabbed the Kyst tightly around the collar. The hunter already had a dagger poking the ribs under his arm.

"Allies?" Ven was tense but still managed to sound friendly. The half-orc looked at the many dead and unconscious travellers around them.

"Allies." His voice was deep and strong. They stood up, and Ven was amazed at the 215 cm height of this fighter. His massive muscles, swollen with adrenalin made his glowering yellow eyes, illuminating a small portion of his brow, appear even more threatening.

"Will the witch's laugh be a problem?" Ven asked. The towering fighter placed his hand where he had been initially hit in the head and knocked out.

"Shouldn't be now. I'm Agan Dusk." He offered his name as if he was reminding himself.

"Ven Devar. Follow me, if you would." The Kyst sprinted back to his party, and Agan was close behind.

Athvar heard the sound of approaching footsteps.

"Ven?" he asked aloud as he was now throwing random items out of his bags in search of something in particular. He squeaked as he triumphantly pulled out a vile of blue liquid. Removing the lid revealed a dropper. He extracted an inexact amount as he rushed to squeeze the potion into Scáth's mouth. When she resisted, Faenla bared his teeth and snarled at her. She took the droplets, and before Athvar pulled his hand away, Scáth was fast asleep. Faenla suddenly gave an ear-piercing yelp as he was slashed in the hip by a possessed traveller. He reared up, twisting and biting hard on the head of his assailant. Landing on his front paws, the sound of neck-snapping echoed as Faenla dropped his prey. Ven and Agan came running through the fog, the lumbering mixed-blood almost tripped over Athvar.

"Hey, watch it, you brainwashed oaf!" Athvar smacked Agan hard in the knee with his mace.

"Ow!" Agan roared painfully.

"Stop! Wait, Athvar, Agan, wait. Allies," Ven said, pleading for the two to pause long enough to hear reason. Agan looked up from the gnome to see the biggest wolf of his life and a peculiar looking unconscious woman.

"These are your travelling companions?" Agan responded with overflowing doubt. He found no response though as Ven rushed to Scáth's side.

"What happened to her?" Ven looked scornfully at Athvar. The tobacco in Athvar's ears meant he couldn't hear well. However, it seemed pretty obvious to Athvar.

"I put her to sleep. Did you kill the witch?" Athvar was yelling as he couldn't hear himself. Ven quickly pressed his index finger to his lips, hushing the gnome. He pointed his finger at Athvar, then down to Scáth. Athvar scurried over and assumed a protective stance over the vulnerable companion. Agan stepped over to Ven and Faenla, who were trying to find the source of the laughter. Neither of them had any luck as it truly sounded like it was coming from every direction.

"What do you propose?" Agan was beginning to doubt his decision to join the elf who had saved him.

"Do you know how to get to the road from here?" Ven questioned without hesitation. Agan shook his head doubtfully. He had lost all sense of direction after being knocked out.

"Any idea how you lure a witch out?" Ven spoke with mostly sarcasm in his voice. However, Agan had a few run-ins with witches over the years and looked to Athvar with keen eyes. Before Athvar knew it, he watched as all three of them disappeared into the mist without a word.

The gnome gave a quiet cry and looked to Scáth. It brought him some comfort to see her resting so peacefully away from this nightmare. Athvar could still hear the muffled laughter of the Bog Witch. He had stuffed so much tobacco in his ears that he was worried he wouldn't be able to get it out again. Yet, he could swear the laughing was growing louder. The gnome looked around nervously; he saw little but wet grass and thick swirling fog. Suddenly the laughing stopped. Surprised as ever, he slowly turned back to face Scáth but instead made direct eye contact with a figure standing roughly twenty paces away. The same drooling, tattered, and leering Bog Witch that had frightened Scáth so greatly.

She ambled toward Athvar, her grin growing wider with each step, unnaturally so. Each step caused more and more brown water to leak between her rotted teeth. He found himself unable to move, unable to break the gaze she held on him. Her laugh was quiet and greedy now, like a child about to devour a slice of cake. Athvar's entire body was trembling under the fear and struggled to break free, to defend himself from this horrid monster. The drool had just begun dripping onto the gnome when Faenla emerged from the fog and leaped a dozen paces to land on the witch. She quickly flicked her hand up in defence, and Faenla collided with an invisible barrier. Agan gave a loud battle cry, letting his emotion fuel his attack. He sent his razor-edged battle-axe twirling at the witch. She flicked her other arm up, causing the axe to stop and reverse direction.

The witch gave a shriek of anger toward Agan as he caught the axe defiantly. The sound of steel penetrating flesh was quickly followed by a hollowed-out moan. The companions watched as Ven's trident burst through the witch's chest. With his other hand, he separated her head from her body with his short sword. What was left of the witch limply fell to the ground. Faenla had slowly got up and walked over to Athvar and Scáth.

"Please forgive me, Athvar, it was the only…" Ven was interrupted by yet another crazed laugh. The gnome was laughing as he had just heard the funniest joke of his life.

"Athvar?" Ven was visibly concerned, and even Faenla let out a whimper as he watched the gnome. Athvar eventually stopped laughing and cleared his throat.

"I'm fine. Can we please leave this place forever?" he stated more than asked as he walked over to the dead witch, kicking her for good measure. Agan looked rather uncomfortable at the gnome's behaviour but understood everyone was affected by these difficult times differently.

Ven gently lifted Scáth off the soggy grass and placed her on Faenla's broad back. It was mid-day now, and the group, including Agan, promptly made their way out of the bog.

With Scáth still heavily asleep on Faenla's back, Athvar was now riding on Ven's shoulders. They made a great team with the added assistance of Agan, in navigating the most efficient route out. Soon, the day's last light suddenly broke the mist as the adventures emerged from a wall of fog nearly a kilometre high and that spanned as far as the eye could see. Before them was a snow-covered region of sparse forests, vast ridges, large lakes, wide rivers, and the Skydore Mountain Range to their right. Everyone breathed in the fresh air and gave a great sigh of relief to be free of the Morass Prairie.

CHAPTER THIRTEEN
Fresh Air

The party broke near a bluff that must have known a lush forest in recent years. The trees were packed densely but left scarred from a fire that had swept through the valley. The coating of snow and ice did offer a unique look against the blackened bark. Agan took up Ven and Athvar's offer of travelling with them until he was feeling right again. He hadn't said anything openly but since awakening from getting struck in the head, with a Kyst elf over him, the half-orc couldn't remember why he was even on the Great Road in the first place. In fact, he couldn't remember much about anything. Athvar had caught Agan completely zoned out several times in the previous hours. As if his mind was on pause and his body was left to idle. However, the gnome had thankfully noted the sporadic disassociation was becoming less frequent as the day progressed.

Agan had brought back enough dried wood to last the entire night and some. Ven had struck a warm fire within minutes, and Faenla had Scáth tightly curled up beside him. He felt every breath the ShadowScorn gave as her upper body slightly tickled his fur with every exhale. The wolf found extreme comfort when any of the adventures fell asleep against him. After the loss of his entire pack at the hands of ambushing Kintar, he yearned for the sensation of belonging. Faenla spent most of his time staring at Ven Devar with puppy-like eyes. What was this unexplainable connection the two hunters shared? The wolf was above average in nearly every regard of its existence. Much like Ven was, yet both of them would give everything that made them unique to have their family back for just one day. Wolves being the pack animals they are, meant Faenla had lost generations of his familial line when the Kintar ambushed them.

Since the fallout with Vakar, Ven had lost what little hope he had of ever finding his birthplace. He wondered every day of his life why he was the only one found on that dinghy by the fishermen of Silva. He was pulled from his worn-out contemplation when Athvar returned, gesturing to a pouch he had just loaded with berries and mushrooms for everyone. No small feat given the stark winter conditions surrounding them. The gnome then went over to Faenla and fed him a small ration of dried meat they kept around just for him on nights where hunting wasn't an option.

"Athvar, how long is she going to sleep for? It's been a full day." Ven looked accusingly toward the gnome.

"Well, I was panicked and the dose wasn't exact," he responded rather sheepishly while feeding Faenla.

"Athvar. How long?" Ven demanded a clear answer.

"Another day!" the gnome blurted out before whispering under his breath. "At the least." Ven sighed heavily and looked over to Scáth. The Kyst did admit to himself, she hadn't looked this peaceful since Hearth. He spotted Agan holding a mushroom up to the moonlight, inspecting it closely.

"What's your story, friend?" Ven asked Agan as he tossed him a piece of salted pork from his own rations. Athvar made a point at the moment to sit, legs crossed next to the fire and eagerly look up at Agan. His big yellow eyes stared back at the pair with intense stoicism.

"Not much to say."

"That is not how sharing a campfire with strangers works. I want to hear something. And make it good," Athvar insisted. Ven gave a smile at Athvar's attitude while never breaking his stare with Agan.

"Once upon a time, my mother was forced upon by a band of elves, who had just succeeded in pillaging and burning an entire village of law-abiding orcs. Moral of the story being, you elves aren't as civilized or enlightened as everyone thinks," he stated blatantly, never breaking eye contact with Ven. The Kyst was not taken aback by the hostility, however. He knew well that all races of Litore were capable of both good and evil. That notion firmly reinforced in his mind as the barbaric Kintar were elves akin to his own kind.

"You hate all elves, I presume?" he asked with genuine honesty.

"Bout as much as you probably hate all orcs."

Athvar sat there wide-eyed in discomfort. "I... was thinking something more of recent years. A good story about encountering bandits on the road or running into a Bog Witch. Heh." He offered a handful of berries uncomfortably. Agan looked to Athvar and began to chuckle casually. Athvar looked to Ven, unsure, and also began to forcibly laugh.

"What about you, little man? Regale me." Agan looked to Athvar without much lustre.

"First off, don't compare gnomes to man, it's rude," Athvar answered indignantly. "Have ya ever been as far west as Serenstrom, Agan?"

Agan thought hard for a moment; his mind still felt like a scrambled egg. Confident in his decision, he simply shook his head.

"I have, some forty years ago now. The entire island is man-made and devoted to the Goddess Sesara. A deity of life and sustenance." Athvar paused and looked to Ven. "In fact, not too long ago. Ven here defended us from three Holy Warriors from the Serenstrom Temple, sent to abduct Scáth, here."

Agan looked to Ven, slightly impressed. "Single handily, might I add. But I digress. It takes nearly a day by longship to get there from the closest mainland dock in Port Noga. The entire city spans nearly fifty kilometres in diameter. The whole place glints like a pearl against sunlight. Given it's the closest civilized land to the 'Unknown Regions', it has become quite a hub for adventures and pioneers seeking riches and fame. The Dawn City in Iridawnia is the only place I've seen that rivals the resplendence of Serenstrom. Unfortunately, since the unexpected birth of Scáth's people, the temple on Serenstrom has declared the Shadow Scorn to be a mockery of their deity."

"And this is why you travel with her now?" Agan asked earnestly.

"I found her lost and alone in the Great Northern Rainforest. She had just escaped her abductors, who planned to sell her in Serenstrom. Athvar and I swore to see her safely returned to the small kingdom of her folk." Ven was eyeing Agan's physical response closely in an effort to understand any intentions this half-orc half-elf may have. Alas, Agan revealed nothing.

"What about you, elf? It's clear you're still a child in the lifespan of your people. I'm surprised they let you out unsupervised." Agan dropped his brow while again not so subtly attacking Ven's heritage. He simply laughed in response, though. Most of Silva's hunters had treated Ven this way. Attempting to elicit some provoked response that could be turned against him. Or, in many cases, so they could duel him to prove they were the better hunter.

"It is true. I am barely through my third decade. However, where I hail from, I had only one supposed equal in fighting prowess," Ven responded evenly and without a hint of spite toward Agan trying to get under his skin.

"This is the 'Mighty Ven Devar.' His skill is legendary in all the Northern Rainforest," Athvar interjected proudly. It was undeniable that the three companions and wolf had grown close from the journey thus far. Athvar, nearing his eighth decade of life, of the typical 10-13 gnomes lived, was feeling pride akin to that of a mentor for Ven. Agan put on an especially unimpressed look.

"What makes you so legendary then, Mighty Devar?" the brooding fighter asked mockingly. Ven recounted the story of his rise to fame for one of the very few times in his life.

"During my twentieth winter, an ice demon crawled its way from the Underworld to the surface. For a month, the Great Northern Rainforest was unrecognizable. Birds solidified mid-flight, dropping from the sky. Trees were coated in thick blue ice, and the ocean waves formed a crust so deep you could walk between the archipelago. The air, so impossibly frigid, that fire itself couldn't sustain to breathe. It was River Luvium, the first and largest Kyst settlement in the north that found the ice demon known as Hoarfrost. They assembled a legion of hunters and sages to destroy the accursed beast. However, I, along with a small troop of Silvan hunters, found the remains of those brave elves, flash frozen where they first encountered the demon. They hadn't even had the chance to break rank before meeting their doom.

"My Queen, Trilara, gathered all the monarchs and assorted leaders of the Northern Kyst. It was decided a single messenger would meet with Hoarfrost to discuss terms. You see, belonging to no one made me expendable in the eyes of many in attendance, save Trilara, who actively voted against my going. Yet, when I volunteered, it was agreed I would speak with the demon. It wasn't hard to find, as a lingering haze of ice fog surrounded the beast for several hundred metres. I tracked it back to a seaside cave, which we later discovered was a direct route to the Underworld. Hoarfrost was large and muscular, supporting its strong upper torso on two impossibly huge arms with two smaller legs bearing its great weight. Demons, above all else, crave chaos and death. It declared that we could choose a champion from each of the main settlements to fight against it, one on one."

"I took the ultimatum back to Silva, and the rulers felt there was little other choice. Six of us went to fight Hoarfrost; Shallowbay, Silva, Sanctuary Island, Red Oak, Geenwave, and River Luvium sent proxy. We met a seventh on the way, as even Claw Canyon sent one of their finest Kintar Berserkers. The hunter from Red Oak fled upon seeing Hoarfrost and all of its exuding terror. The sages from Sanctuary Island and Shallowbay wrought a display of arcane might I have yet to see matched. The hunter from Greenwave had his arms and legs frozen while using his bow. I'll never forget his cries as Hoarfrost devoured him alive. The Berserker lasted the longest and dealt many seemingly harmless cuts to the demon, but alas, she was splattered against the seawall by an immense icy fist. I stood in front of the unfazed demon, utterly humbled by its sheer supremacy. I knew I would meet a fate similar to those before me, and to my surprise, I was okay with that. I gripped my trident and short sword, convincing myself I would die honourably. A sudden and surprisingly warm gust of wind blew across the frozen ocean to rustle my cloak. Carried on that breeze were softly whispered words that tickled my ear and said, "Salt to the heart."

"I didn't feel particularly confident in those words, for the only salt available was under an arms length of ice. I immediately went into a series of dodges while goading Hoarfrost on. Eventually it broke the ice, and I dipped my trident into the salt water before hurling it forthwith. The razor-sharp points sank in but not deep enough, acting on instinct, I sent my sword spinning for its face. Distracted by the thrown weapon, I sprinted and jumped into a butterfly kick, connecting my leading foot with the pommel to embed the trident deep into Hoarfrost's chest. It could have killed me still, for it slowly melted from the inside out. Instead, it said in abject shock and delight, "It is you," before eventually dispersing into a cloud of ice particles, summoned back through the cave tunnel."

"See, that's how ya tell a campfire story!" Athvar said proudly, as he had never heard the famous tale spoken of from Ven, nor in such detail.

Agan simply scoffed at the Kyst's story.

"Hey! Ya owe him respect for even sharing-"

"-Athvar," Ven politely interrupted. "It's fine. He asked; I answered."

Agan made a point of rolling his eyes at the elf taking the high road.

"You don't remember, do you?" Ven questioned, already knowing the answer but remaining sympathetic.

"What?" He spat back.

"After you woke up from being hit in the head. I've seen it before. You don't remember what you were doing out here, even now, do you?" Ven offered a way out for Agan by bringing up what the half-orc was too proud too. Athvar looked back to Agan and thought it made perfect sense now. It certainly explained why he had seen the brooding fellow look so lost throughout the day.

Agan was caught off guard by the Kyst's astute observation. Between the intensive climbing, hunting, and defending their land from hostiles, Ven had witnessed all kinds of peculiar side effects of suffering head wounds. Feeling grumpy and far more tired than normal, Agan gave in and admitted it.

"You are correct. Forgive my anger toward you. My head is—" Trying to find the right words, Ven interrupted.

"—I know. Worry not, friend. Rest easy tonight, and tomorrow you will feel far better." He threw Agan a heavy blanket as he said so.

"Thank you." He nodded appreciatively. Agan laid down, shoulders and head propped up against a log. Athvar soon fell asleep near the fire as well, leaving Ven Devar awake. Even Faenla was uncharacteristically passed out after the arduous three days of fog. The hunter knew he had another night and day in him before needing to rest, so he happily took watch.

It was beautiful up here, he thought. They had settled near the top of a ridge that overlooked a great valley. Ven could see for kilometres as the snow sparkled like diamonds against the moonlight. A large river flowed through the basin of the valley, refusing to yield to winter's frozen touch. It continued to spew fresh glacier water into Litore Lake, the single largest land-locked body of water on the continent.

CHAPTER FOURTEEN

Betrayal Grows in Trust

The residents of Hearth were experiencing an intense wave of mourning for the late Queen Ilthanis Veldove. The entire village of both Kyst and gnomes were in attendance for her funeral, including the refugees of Silva. They were all adorned in large, flowing robes and stood neatly along the beach. Every single attendee held a candle of flickering, green flame with a seashell base. Under the moonlight of the clear sky, the raging winter ocean and rushing white caps were easily seen. Two looming and detailed statues of Āina and Kaia watched over the open casket. Four sages stood over the deceased Ilthanis, giving prayer in their native language of Kystin to their God and Goddess. Vakar walked over to the elegantly carved and open casket holding Ilthanis. He knelt beside it and planted a kiss on her forehead before weakly whispering.

"This shall not be in vain." He placed his hand on the oiled cedar and muttered an incantation. Lifting his hand revealed a soft glowing rune pulsing with energy. Soon after, the casket lifted from the pebbles and floated out over the ocean. So too did the candles follow, as if a gust of wind had just swept them from everyone's grasp. Queen Ilthanis looked as divine as she ever had as she floated over the ocean, surrounded by her own sea of lambent flame. The gathered watched in silence as the candles and casket were consumed by a single towering wave. All the Kyst gave a quiet but collective gasp, assured the wave was sent by Kaia, Goddess of the Sea, welcoming Ilthanis to the next world.

Vakar was the last one on the beach. With his knees bent to his chest, he watched the birth of another dawn. It was deep into the night when he granted himself permission to weep. He was truly and eternally remorseful for the murder of Ilthanis. He had grown undeniably fond of her in the recent weeks. No matter how much Vakar wished otherwise, life was simply too far gone to return back to the way things were before the fire. He fully intended to see Silva and its people returned to their former glory. He had sworn over the grave of both Qiri and now Ilthanis that he would not stop there. It became clear to him that the sages and hunters from Silva and Hearth combined made for a force to be reckoned with. They could accomplish much under the right leadership, which currently both parties were craving. He could ensure peace and safety to all Kyst in the Great Northern Rainforest if they pledged to acknowledge Vakar 'The Cunning' as their king. The first king of all Northern Kyst. Now that he could successfully lead his people unopposed, he needed a cause that could unify the other tribes under one banner.

Rexous was currently in a small oaken room that glowed a soft yellow from fire light. The Kyst sat on his fur-lined bed, legs crossed and in deep meditation. The popping and hissing of steam escaping wood crept into his subconscious. Taking him back to that night when his home was transformed into a burning nightmare of anguish and death. His own kin and citizens, slaughtered in their beds, cut down protecting their children and elderly. Kind and caring Kyst, undeserving of such real terror brought on by the raiding Kintar. Through his meditation, he re-lived the experiences over and over again. Protecting his mother and queen. Struggling to free himself from the razor-sharp talons of the Giant-Raptor. Plummeting over a thousand metres through the entire forest canopy. Whipped relentlessly by cedar sprays, ricocheted bodily off wide, unyielding branches. Crawling back to his dead mother's side, battered and profusely bleeding with the stench of death already nipping at him. At last, the sweet moment when he slipped that dagger into Ven Devar.

The former prince was awoken from his meditation by three loud and distinct knocks on his door. Getting out of bed, he draped a long black robe with golden leaves embroidered across the shoulders. Still on his guard, he held a reverse-gripped dagger in one hand that was concealed under his loose sleeve. Opening the door and seeing only a familiar face, he immediately spun around and went to stand near the heat of the fire.

"How do your wounds heal?" Uthul asked with keen interest.

"Painfully. Which has me thinking on our agreement." Rexous half leaned against the hearth and half-faced Uthul, who was just now raising a brow at the confident prince.

"Go on."

"In simply killing the 'Mighty Ven Devar', I am not avenging my mother. To do so, I must destroy the legend he has already become. You know as well as I, there are hundreds of pocket settlements of Kyst up and down the coast. Including some that have outgrown what Silva was."

The listening Uthul poured wine into two glasses. "Your proposal?"

"We poison his name." Rexous spat vehemently. Uthul smiled, handing him the wine. "We can launch a series of targeted assaults on Kyst communities. I will pose as the Mighty Hunter and wreak havoc just long enough to make it known that Ven Devar truly is the traitor who wrought the destruction of Silva. Only then, once all the Great Northern Rainforest has grown to hate his legacy, will I kill him." By the time Rexous finished, his heart was racing from the animosity that was linked to the words. Uthul, who usually wore his heart on his sleeve, was smiling in disbelief.

He raised his glass toward Rexous. "Too brilliant ideas."

"And new partnerships." Rex scowled as he clinked glasses with his mother's murderer.

The macer and Igon sat in the highest turret of the Sesara Temple. It was a chamber of extravagance reserved for the leader of their faith. Several windows gave light to the room and offered breathtaking panoramic views. Above was an enormous diamond chandelier that fragmented the light of ever-burning candles, showering the room in a rainbow of hues. The walls were strewn with many bookshelves that had arcane chains strung along each shelf. The two counsel members watched as a wizard was finishing a complex pentagram with charcoal on a vacant spot of the stone wall. It slightly resembled that of a door but was filled with geometric lines and patterns. The wizard stood in front of the now completed portal and bowed separately to the macer and Igon before leaving the chamber. A moment later, the whole pentagram on the wall began glowing a vibrant green. It grew in luminance until the marbled wall beneath the charcoal was nothing more than a swirling portal. Out from it stepped two regal and proud Kyst elves.

Uthul immediately saw the scowl on Igon's face, so he quickly bowed low to the humans. Rexous, on the other hand, did no such thing. Remaining tall and confident as he looked at the men with heavy eyes and one brow raised. He undoubtedly thought they looked too fat and comfortable in their high tower.

"Allow me to introduce Rexous. Former Prince of Silva," Uthul eagerly announced.

"What is the meaning of this uninvited guest, Uthul? Who does not even bow before the Benevolent Macer of Sesara," Igon protested. Uthul looked taken aback by the hostility, but then Rexous fully placed his disarming stare upon the plump man. All the while, O'Donnell was interested to see how things would play out. The tall, slender, and extremely dangerous Kyst, sidled up in front of Igon. Looking down at the man, Rexous did not blink until Igon was literally bumping against the table to get away. Once that was accomplished, Rexous turned to the Macer and gave a brief unceremonious bow.

"I've been informed we have common interests," Rexous said amiably to the Macer while giving a side-eye to Igon.

"What has Uthul told you?" Macer responded while looking accusingly at Uthul.

"He wishes to join us, Your Benevolence," Uthul answered for Rex with great respect. Macer O'Donnell eyed Rexous curiously.

"I wish to kill a particular Kyst who travels to ShadowScorn," Rexous stated firmly.

"I have no interest in killing Kyst," the Macer replied indifferently.

"No?" Rexous feigned surprise. "Well, you wish to finally sack ShadowScorn, do you not?"

"You told him too much!" Igon spat the words at Uthul. The leader of Sesara turned his all-powerful stare upon his zealous colleague.

"Out," was all the Macer said to Igon, who immediately dropped his head in shame and briskly exited. Now it was just the three of them, and O'Donnell went to pour his visitors a strangely thick liquor. The young elf sidled up next to a large window that overlooked the eastern side of Serenstrom. The sky was without a cloud, and Rex was surprised when he spotted Litore far off in the distance.

"Rexous here is known as one of the finest warriors in the Great Rainforest. In particular, his battle strategies are unparalleled. He led many great defences against raiding Kintar and lingering monsters." Uthul was trying hard to make his new ally seem of usefulness to the Macer. Macer wanted to comment on the poor defence of Silva, and the lack of status Rex now held, but managed to stay his tongue.

"Impressive. Though I assure you, we have enough battle-proven generals to lead our thousands. However, our assassins proved useless when they encountered this 'Ven Devar' you seek. Perhaps you will fare better in their stead?" Macer's suggestion was the best Uthul could have hoped for. Rexous thought he would cut ties with the Sesara believers once this was done. Unless he ended up taking a liking to the role of assassin, in which case he might kill the Macer just to shake things ups. One thing at a time, he reminded himself.

"When do you plan to strike?" Rexous asked brazenly. Macer looked to Uthul in disbelief at the forwardness of this particular elf.

"Six weeks time," he managed to answer politely.

"Good. And I trust you can get us there quickly?" Rexous looked to Uthul as he spoke. "We have things to attend to in the forest first." Uthul nodded to Rex in agreeance with his plan. The Macer gave a small but affirming nod of his head. Rexous bowed much lower than he initially had done.

"Then we will see you in six weeks." Rex looked to Uthul and walked back through the portal while dawning his hood.

O'Donnell turned his amused gaze toward the remaining elf. "He does not know?"

"Of course not," Uthul said with a devilish grin.

"Continue the good work." The Macer tossed a leather satchel, filled to the draw string with diamonds and rubies. Uthul gave a respectful bow and typical cocky wink before he too disappeared through the portal.

As Uthul emerged, he saw his fifty-best Kintar Berserkers standing in rows of ten on the forest floor. Ahead of them was Rexous, wearing a dark PumaSheep cloak, a longbow and quiver around his shoulder.

Uthul noted a trident strapped to his hip and a short sword around his tailbone. He was truly taken aback by how much Rexous resembled Ven Devar, even down to the posture. 'The Betrayer' stood above his forces, ready to address the battle-hungry elves.

"This here is Ven Devar. Once your fiercest enemy, now your greatest ally. Follow his every word, and I promise all the spoils of war will be yours." His voice boomed in the guttural language of the Kintar. The Berserkers looked to each other, unsure about following such a hated enemy into battle. One brooding raider, with more scars and festering wounds than thought possible on a living creature, spoke up moronically in his native tongue.

"I'll never take orders from a flowery Kyst. Better we use his skin for clothes, meat for food, and bones for weapons!" A group of nearly ten Kintar erupted in roars of agreement. In a flash, the inciting Kintar was suddenly silenced as arrow fletchings protruded from his mouth, and the arrow-head exploded out the base of his skull. The rest of the Kintar promptly resumed their initial silence. Rexous dropped his shooting stance and slung the bow over his shoulder again.

"As I said." Uthul, motioned for Rexous to take command. Wasting no time, he started a sprint through the forest, with the Kintar following close behind.

The evening was young; twilight's waning colour was nearly drained from the horizon. The Kyst fishermen of a small village on the western edge of the rainforest were just beginning to find their way home for the night. A bitterly-cold rain pounded the coastal village that was built upon a Seacliff.

Rexous looked down on the village from a sturdy arbutus trunk. He knew there would only be a few sages and hunters to speak of in such a small settlement. He laid eyes on a group of Kyst that sat around a communal fire in the centre of town. He knocked a single arrow, drew his aim and held it for a tense moment. To fire the arrow meant taking the life of an innocent. He had never dreamt of committing such a heinous crime, and now he stood at the point of no return. Rex accepted the person he had been was burned along with Silva, and understood what was required to achieve vengeance. His fingers barely relaxed, and the arrow whistled through the rain and found its target, drilling into the spine of one unlucky citizen. The others around the fire were falling over themselves at the sight of their dead comrade. They began fumbling to their homes when the horrifying Kintar roar echoed from the forest. Rexous leaped from the tree into the centre of town and began chopping down anyone he could see, with trident and short sword in hand. He was surpassed by a flood of Berserker's, whooping cries of battle as they joined the slaughter. They went to torching whatever they could, killing everyone in their path. Rexous kept his hood low and quickly went to find the hunters and sages of the settlement. He spotted one hunter emerging from what would have been an insignificant cabin if not for the humble statues of a hunter and sage overlooking the entrance.

Rexous fired an arrow, and the hunter hit the ground, dead without evening knowing what killed him. The Ven Devar imposter burst through the doors of the hall. He instantly dived into a roll as a blast of smouldering hot energy sent by a sage blew the door off its hinges. Rexous felt the heat wave ripple by as he threw a dagger into the heart of the sage. A sinister grin consumed his face when he heard one of the hunters yell in fright.

"It's the Mighty Ven Devar!"

Rexous unsheathed his sword once more, coming into a low defensive stance, much like Ven was known for. He had watched and trained with the 'Mighty Hunter' his whole life and was confident in his movements. He caught an incoming sword strike from a hunter with his trident. Another blast emitted from a sage behind him, Rex dropped low, letting the blast connect squarely with the hunter he was duelling. That unfortunate Kyst collapsed into a pile of ash. He quickly twisted his torso in the direction of the blast, releasing his short sword to soar the three-metre gap into the chest of the unfortunate sage. He dipped his back low, nearly touching the floor to avoid a scimitar swing aimed at his throat. The hunter wielding it came around and down, but Rexous, on his back now, compressed his legs to his chest and kicked out hard. A guttural noise escaped the lips of the hunter kicked in the gut as he landed hard on his arse. He looked up to see what he thought was Ven Devar, a hero and legend, throwing a dagger to end his life. By now, the screaming outside the hall had subsided. A large Kintar who was leading the raiders approached the Kyst, who was now standing over several of his own dead kind.

"The folk here are all dead. Save one as requested, Ven Devar," the bald and grotesque-looking Berserker said proudly. Although he could not see it, Rexous had heavy streaks of tears running down his face, cutting lines through the splattered blood.

"To the next one." His words chilled, void of any emotion.

CHAPTER FIFTEEN
The Hunted

The sound of her heavy cloak flapping in the wind as she ran was all the feral needed to track the ShadowScorn woman. All ferals were once humanoids but now disgusting hybrids. They are an organization of cultists known throughout Litore for their unhealthy obsession with nature. They underwent rituals described only as 'disturbing to the soul' that could transform these followers into mutated forms of their chosen animal. Gaining significant advantages but often at the cost of their sanity. This feral in particular favoured the wolf.

Scáth ran through the forest of sparse trees with red bark and vanilla white leaves. Her breath was ragged, lungs unable to keep up with the pace required to barely outrun the feral chasing her. She had been collecting firewood when the wretched beast emerged to attack her. Losing her scimitar in a brief skirmish after lodging it into the feral's bicep, she had no choice but to let go and run. The not-so-distant howling had far too much human voice in it, motivating her to flee even faster. She heard the heavy footfalls of the feral running on all four legs, gaining ground quickly. It was all too familiar, she thought. Running through the forest, helpless and afraid. The feral was nipping at her ankles now, any second she knew it would have her.

Scáth gave a ringing scream as Faenla jumped straight out of a bush, over her and onto the feral. She threw herself into the snow so as not to be knocked out by her soaring companion. Vicious growls and snarls could be heard as Faenla landed directly onto the monster. The two beasts came out of a barrel role, Faenla standing now between Scáth and the feral, gave a long howl, alerting Ven of his whereabouts. The feral opened its wide craw, revealing two rows of yellow canine and human teeth. The monstrosity weighed much less than the natural wolf but was far more agile and manoeuvrable; favouring a wolf's speed but maintaining its human posture. Faenla circled for a split second before leaping, paws out to bat the feral's head down. His paws connected with the grotesque-looking face, digging deep gashes across it. The feral swung his arm into the ribcage of the alpha. Faenla yelped, reared back up on his hind legs and snapped his powerful jaw on the feral's snout, tearing a clean chunk from his face. The feral gave a great shriek of pain before punching the alpha in throat and biting off the tip of Faenla's right ear. The alpha's entire body recoiled in pain and, in one instinctive and savage bite, broke the monster's neck. Scáth slowly turned over to see Faenla on all fours, sniffing at the limply twitching feral. Assured it was dead, he used his front right paw to gently and repetitively swipe at his injured ear.

He refrained when Scáth wrapped her arms tightly around his thick mane. Burying her face deep in his warm, comforting fur, Faenla rested his head on her shoulder, gently nuzzling his companion. After a moment of respite, she heard her other three companions come barreling out of the same bush, weapons ready. She rubbed her face in his fur and stood up, as did Faenla, who went back to smelling the dead feral. Ven ran to Scáth while Agan and Athvar joined Faenla by the dead beast.

"Damn, we missed the fun," Agan said while planting a boot on the beast's forearm and yanking out Scáth's scimitar.

"She was lucky to have ya!" Athvar said to Faenla as he put an ointment on the tip of the wolf's missing ear. Athvar continued to speak to Faenla as if he was fully engaged in conversation. "True, but yar lucky it wasn't more of the ear!" the gnome said, laughing. Agan couldn't help but give the little guy a funny look before he walked over to Scáth and Ven.

"A rhetorical lesson, Lady Scáth." Agan handed her the scimitar. "Don't ever leave your weapon. Ever."

"Thanks," she replied with dry sarcasm. Ven laughed at Agan's attempt at humour, but they both knew Scáth was making excellent progress with her training. Ven and Agan had been spending one hour each day with Scáth, sharing their knowledge of combat and war. However, it was obvious to both veterans that the ShadowScorn was unparalleled in stealth. So they decided Scáth would focus on the skills of a rogue or spy. The Kyst spent close to a month since exiting the fog on hand-to-hand combat with the Scorn. While Agan taught lessons of tactics and understanding your opponent, all things he learned the hard way during his time as a mercenary and guild leader.

The group eventually found their way back to camp with firewood in hand. Athvar and Agan were seated around the comforting flames while Ven and Scáth worked on basic swordplay.

"Have ya decided if ya'll join us the rest of the way? I can only imagine few outsiders in history have seen the inside of ShadowScorn," Athvar asked Agan while munching on his evening rations. The half-orc kept his gaze on the fire, poking at it with a long stick.

"I don't have much choice. I fear if my memory does not return, I will not know where to go or what to do." Agan seemed more distant than usual. He hadn't been overly chatty since joining them on their journey, which the group chalked up to being his normal behaviour, but something was different from even that.

"What's the last thing you do remember?" Athvar looked at him with a concern that Agan felt to be genuine.

"I've recollected what I believe to be the most recent. I served as a sell-sword for the Dragon-bloods of Rhogar against the Dwarves of Silver Rock." Agan pulled out a signet from his satchel given to him by King Dusanith of Rhogar. "Maybe I was heading to the next job."

Athvar wore a worried look. "Rhogar and the Dwarves of Silver Rock have been peaceful for nearly ten years," he said with a heavy heart.

Agan's expression didn't change as he continued to stoke the fire.

"Perhaps, if you're memory has not returned, Lady Scáth could have a haler in ShadowScorn help you," Athvar offered with a sudden change of positivity.

"Are all gnomes as optimistic as you?" Agan asked cynically.

"Yup!" Athvar replied instantly and with furthered enthusiasm. Agan chuckled slightly, which made Athvar feel more at ease. He didn't necessarily trust Agan, he was always brooding, and the gnome could never tell if the half-orc liked him or wanted to kick him.

In a red-stained, snow-filled ditch lay the torn-up remnants of the werewolf feral. Three other of the monstrosities were currently sniffing their dead comrade in the early hours. A tall woman had small hairs covering her skin with a long thick tail trailing her. She was that of a cougar, with dense and tightly wound muscles. The other two ferals weighed nearly 450 kilograms each and stood roughly three metres tall. They were of bear blood with huge snouts and massive paws. The feral pack wasted little time in tracking the scent of the party.

The adventurers got an early start the next day as they were expecting to reach a ferry that would take them across Litore Lake. They were surrounded by small jagged mountains as they trekked through the snow powdered, river-fed valley. Glistening clear glacier water flowed southeast before spilling into the lake. Tall grass miraculously sprouted through the snow and was topped with budding flowers. Athvar was in his customary position on the back of Faenla when the majestic wolf suddenly lurched to a halt in front of everyone. No one made a sound as it was obvious he was trying to detect the presence of something. Faenla fluttered his ears to the left and then to the right.

"Ven," whispered Agan.

"What?"

"I see something to our right flank," Agan said, nodding in that direction. Ven studied it for a moment and saw nothing.

"I don't."

"To our left," Scáth said quietly. Ven looked to their left and saw what he thought was the tale-end of a bear. Faenla lowered his head, looking behind the group and bared his teeth.

"How far to the crossing, Athvar?" Ven considered they could run the distance.

"Thirty minutes, an hour? Hard to say," the gnome replied. Ven looked to Scáth as she appeared to be holding eye contact with something. Ven began to feel out of his element, and a sudden wave of doubt took control of his mind. He could feel the creatures surrounding them, the hideous intent of their minds. He looked to

Agan with worried eyes.

"We run. Run until we must fight." Agan gleamed with confidence.

"One... two... three!" Athvar shouted, already tightly grasping his rope harness. Faenla shot forward with astounding speed, leaving the elf, Scorn, and half-orc to fend for themselves. Ven ran with his Kyst crafted bow at the ready, two arrows knocked at all times. If he got the chance, it would only take the flick of a finger to adjust one arrow for a second target. Agan began to slightly take the lead with his far bigger frame and mighty steps. Scáth tucked neatly into the middle with her scimitar in hand, knowing in broad daylight she'd be at a disadvantage without lingering shadow to call upon. Much to Athvar's dismay, Faenla only shot forward ahead of the group so he could double back and flank the pursuing ferals.

Ven eventually caught sight of the feral cougar effortlessly leaping through the trees alongside them. He looked forward as he heard Agan give a boisterous battle cry and run headlong into a feral bear who had just emerged from the bushes in front of them. Ven fired two arrows at the feral cougar, missing their mark but causing her to slip off the branch and tumble. The feral bear stood up tall and dropped his entire weight on the charging Agan. It gave a bellowing roar of defiance as he dropped his mangled paws onto the fighter. The half-orc was unyielding, digging his boots into the dirt, pushing the bear back with his powerful torso. Scáth and Ven couldn't believe their eyes. Agan repeatedly jabbed his battle-axe into the feral's belly without mercy. He didn't stop until he heard the sound of an arrow piercing the skull of the beast. He shoved it off to the side and kept running with his companions.

"I lost sight of one!" Ven yelled while the group kept a steady pace.

"I as well!" Scáth declared with an even breath.

"Where's your damn wolf run off too, Devar?" Agan shouted accusingly.

"He belongs to no one! Do you ever think with the elven half of your brain?" Ven laughed to himself when he looked past Scáth to see Agan was too winded to reply. He hadn't worried for a moment about Faenla's disappearance. He knew the wolf would never leave the group defenceless. The trio was now running through two rows of trees whose leaves had grown together above, forming a natural tunnel. The group skidded to a stop when the light at the other end of the pathway was blotted out by the remaining feral bear. Ven looked behind them and spotted the feral cougar, now walking on two legs, putting one in front of the other in a seductive swing of her hips. Tail swaying back and forth in delight.

"Now what?" Agan growled through gritted teeth. Ven quickly stepped past Agan with his bow in hand. He readied his stance and knocked three arrows at a time. Within the span of a few seconds, Ven launched a dozen arrows into the feral bear, who then proceeded to fall face-first into the frozen ground. They simultaneously spun their heads as they heard the feral cougar give a screech that resembled a woman's sorrowful scream far more than normal.

"We keep running!" Ven yelled, already grasping Scáth's hand on the run. Agan didn't waste any time chasing after his companions. Faenla wasn't thirty seconds behind the trail of the pursuing feral. They barely slowed down to glance at the bear that was filled with arrows at the far end of the path.

"Well done, Ven," Athvar muttered to himself as they passed the corpse. The group of fleeing adventurers saw the sky open up as they came around a bend that displayed a small shack with a dock and ship on the edge of the lake.

"Who are they?" Scáth shouted with worry before either of her comrades even noticed the small group of men standing around the shack. A lone human sailor, only clad in undergarments, was bent over on his knees, shivering in the freezing climate. The party could barely halt before they were only a few dozen strides from the group of men. The captain of these men had chiselled features and a sly smile. He wore long tabards over his ornate black and red plate armour. He turned to regard the approaching group, as did all seven of his soldiers, three of them aiming crossbows their way. The captain's look of surprise quickly faded into an eerily pleased expression. In quick pursuit, the feral cougar came sprinting around the corner, eyes locked on her prey. In perfect coordination, the three crossbowmen shot their bolts at the beast. Each finding their intended mark, sending the creature skidding several metres limply through the snow.

"Huh huh, looks like he was telling the truth, Captain." The largest of the soldiers spoke with uncivilized stupidity. Ven immediately recognized the symbol of Sesara painted on the captain's armour. A lush and bountiful landscape with a stag and doe looking inwards while grazing next to a river. The image, enwrapped in an almost kite-shield shape. He noted several of the men to be wearing pendants around their necks of the same symbol.

"Cut me red, I was wrong. We were under the impression this worm had ferried you across the lake already," the captain said while nonchalantly stepping behind the shivering sailor.

"What do you want?" Ven's voice echoed across the water with authority. The captain looked at the elf with dark, soulless, brown eyes. The Kyst could tell this man had been through many hardships in his day. Ultimately creating the jaded and coarse human before them. Ven's passing thought was proven true as the captain held out his hand to the nearest crossbowman. The soldier promptly surrendered the weapon to his leader, already cocked and loaded. The captain placed the weapon against the sailor's head and let loose. The bolt emerged through the sailor's forehead to paint the snow.

"Look at her boys." As he crudely waved the crossbow in Scáth's direction. "She's prettier than the boss let on." His men all chuckled lewdly, staring uncomfortably at the ShadowScorn. Ven began to feel that unbridled rage boil inside. The sheer injustice of murdering the sailor and horrid insinuations made toward Scáth was far more than it took for him to lose control. His teeth gnashed, and his knuckles whitened.

"You are from the Church of Sesara, yes?" Agan enthusiastically piped in while taking a large step forward. The captain and his men set their gaze upon the hulking half-orc half-elf fighter. "As am I." He pulled a gold chained symbol of Sesara from under his armour. The captain raised his eyebrows in humour.

"She works in funny ways, does she not?" the captain stated more than asked. His crew of soldiers laughed, and Agan joined in emphatically, taking another step toward the captain.

"She most certainly does, Captain. It's an honour to meet one of your rank. Oh! Look, I must show you this." Agan began reaching under a large red sash that went around his belly. "I picked it up from the only Sesara Temple in Rhogar." The captain, uninterested, turned back to his soldiers, giving them a signal to ready up. As the captain turned back to Agan, his head was violently struck and twisted 180-degrees. The captain's eyes were still wide as his head was now facing his men. His face and back hit the snow just as Agan threw the small warhammer at one of the crossbowmen. It connected with the throat of his target, causing him to drop to his knees, making a sick coughing noise.

"Roundup!" one of the men shouted, but he was fast silenced with a dagger to the heart from Ven. The five men still heeding the battle call formed a tight line and moved as a unit. Their shields made them tough targets, and every few seconds, the one remaining crossbowman would pop over the shield wall and fire a bolt at the adventurers. Ven flicked his trident up in front of his face with a twirl. He felt a pressure and gripped the handle firmly, seeing it had caught the crossbow bolt. A howl was heard echoing from the forest, then Faenla leaped out from the tree line, jumping once, twice, and thrice, before landing on the entire shield wall, scattering the soldiers. Faenla bit down on the biggest man, easily wrapping his razor-sharp fangs around the entire head.

Agan gave a powerful battle cry and cleaved his double-bearded axe with a furious might across the back of one fumbling soldier. Scáth courageously ran toward the left flank and prevented the crossbowman from getting a shot-off on Faenla. She sliced her scimitar clean through the man's wrist, severing his hand that still gripped the falling crossbow. She caught it and fired it right into the underside of his chin. Agan was in the upswing of cutting the last soldiers head off when Ven shouted.

"Wait!" Throwing his hand up toward the hulking fighter, Agan brought his axe down anyway, separating the head from the body with a single chop. Ven's heart skipped a beat with rage.

"Hey!" the elf rushed up and yelled in Agan's face. When Agan just scoffed and turned his back to the Kyst, Ven saw only red. He kicked the back of Agan's knee, dropping the fighter and drove his sword pommel into the back of his head.

"Answers, we need answers!" Ven shouted at the half-orc in the snow. Just then, Athvar walked out from the bushes to witness the altercation.

Agan jumped up and deftly spun, jamming his axe handle into Ven's nose. The Kyst's face spurted blood, and he landed hard, knocking the wind from him. Agan stared at Ven with murderous intent, and Ven was not about to back down. Before either of them could make the next move, Scáth and Athvar were between them.

"That's enough!" the Scorn fearlessly shouted at both warriors.

"Control yourself, elf. Lest something bad befalls you," Agan threatened.

"He's in the right, Agan," Athvar boldly interjected. "You kill without mercy, and we are desperate for information."

Scáth helped Ven to his feet, and Athvar walked the half-orc away. Ven's anger washed away, and he felt a sense of regret as he looked at the Scorn giving him a disappointed stare. Ven went over to check the captain's body for any possible information. If he hadn't seen it for himself, he would not have believed Agan really twisted the man's head around with a single swing from something barely bigger than a carpenter's hammer. Athvar went over to one of the bodies and took a large step back in shock.

"Scáth, please tell me it wasn't Sesaran soldiers that abducted ya. If that were the case—"

"—It would mean the City of Shadow will soon see another war with the Church of Sesara," Scáth finished the gnome's line of thought. Ven looked at her with a degree of accusation.

"Surely you would have told us if you knew?" the Kyst asked with a slightly wounded ego.

"Of course I did not know. The men who took me were sell-swords. But who else would have the resources to break into my city, my home, and steal me away undetected?" The group remained silent at her realism. Ven found nothing on the captain but a satchel of gold, which he threw in Athvar's direction. Under the breastplate, the Kyst did find a secret pocket actually built into the armour. It was a letter written by the Arch Priest of Renrit, instructing the captain to 'not engage with the ShadowScorn elf or her protectors. Return with haste to Renrit once the targets have been spotted so we may ready our march.'

Agan seemed unbothered by the realization they were being hunted by one of the most powerful religions in Litore. He continued to make his round to each fallen soldier, looting what valuables he could.

"Them not returning is as good as them confirming our arrival. We should not waste any more time," Ven said, walking over to the small dock where a single mast sailboat was moored. Scáth couldn't have agreed more and was right behind him. Faenla walked over with them but took his sweet time sniffing the dock and boat before he ever so cautiously placed his front paws onto the taffrail and leaped in. Athvar went over to Agan, who had been at the same body for several minutes, staring blankly.

"Agan?" he said to the half-elf softly. Agan didn't respond verbally or physically, utterly motionless while staring at the body. The soldier wasn't anything unique; a middle-aged human with a dagger hilt protruding his chest.

"Agan." Athvar was far more authoritative, trying to snap his companion out of it. Agan looked to Athvar, surprised by the gnome's presence and quickly looked back to the body. Athvar looked up to Ven and Scáth, who were preparing the ship.

"He looks... familiar." Agan's words escaped like a fleeting thought. A loud whistle was heard, and the pair turned their gaze to Ven standing on the stern of the boat. The hunter motioned for them to join and turned back to help Scáth unfurl the sail. Athvar placed a hand on the half-elf's knee, beckoning him to follow. Agan did so without complaint. Even picking up the gnome and throwing him on his left shoulder in a playful manner.

"Excuse me, please ask before picking up a gnome," Athvar jokingly scolded the half-orc.

"My deepest apologies," Agan offered with sincerity. The two shared a hardy laugh and proceeded to the sailboat that would ferry them on their last leg of the journey.

CHAPTER SIXTEEN
Belonging

When I was a boy, those who knew me claimed I would be a great warrior. I did not grow up like many of the other Kyst I served with. From a babe, I lived in the hunter's hall, among the already fully-trained and initiated. A hunter known as Renic Devar took wardship over me until I was ten years of age. One unforgettable day, Renic and I were accompanied by three other hunters on a routine border check. I had eventually veered off our assigned path, which I was constantly berated for. I felt the sense of something in danger at the time; unsure of what it meant or what it even was, I followed the feeling. Soon, I stumbled upon a quintet of Kintar surrounding a lone goblin. They muttered drooling words of eating the wretched thing alive. I instinctively drew my bow, remembering Renic's teachings and let loose into the temple of one salivating Kintar. All four of the raiders turned their frightening visage upon me, and being the mere child I was, I froze in place. I gave a loud shriek of terror when the goblin, nearly the same height I was at the time, looked at me with his big sour yellow eyes and beady black pupils. One of the Kintar bashed the goblin in the shoulder with a boneclub, hurling the creature into a tree. Another Kintar approached, grabbing me by the scruff of my neck and hoisting me up to eye level. "Little Kyst tastes good." Spittle drenched my face as he threatened me in my own language. He entirely licked my left cheek before a trident came soaring from nowhere, embedding itself deep into the raider's ribcage. Renic jumped up and off the side of one tree, onto then off a second before plunging his short sword deep into the chest of one slow-reacting Kintar. I will always remember seeing my mentor and protector leaping between those trees onto his prey, killing it swiftly before rolling forward into a low-readied defensive stance. Heroically throwing himself into mortal danger to save me. The Kintar holding me roared with terrifying ferocity in my face as he pulled the trident from his ribcage. Before he could harm me, a short sword struck his back, a face of shock replaced the anger. The nearly 160-kilogram Kintar fell atop me, pinning me to the ground. Forcing me to helplessly watch as Renic faced off with the three remaining raiders. They were massive beasts, and Renic was now without any primary weapon. He held a dagger reverse grip in each hand, calmly regaining his focus while standing in the middle of the encircling adversaries. They each gave a roar of defiance, even Renic, as they one, two, then three charged at the lone hunter. Renic threw a dagger at the first and closest of them, hitting its mark in the sprinting raider's shoulder. The Kyst leaped forward, grabbing onto the dagger and swinging up onto the Kintar's shoulders. To my utter amazement, Renic wrapped his legs around the brute's neck and threw himself forward. Causing the hulking raider to do a full flip, landing hard on his back with Renic still firmly squeezing his neck with his thighs. The other two Kintar swung down but were too slow. The Mighty Hunter rolled back, causing one Kintar to strike dirt while the other accidentally drove his jagged axe deep into the prone raider's skull. Renic now stood proud in front of the other two, beckoning them forth. They answered by giving their terrifying battle cries and springing forward. Before either of them took their second step, two whistling arrows caught them in their throats. Sent by the hunters of Silva who had just caught up to Renic and myself. I felt an immense release of pressure as my saviour pushed the brute off, stood me upright, and embraced me tightly. I hugged him tighter than I had ever hugged anyone before or since. In that split second, I felt as though I had a father. Someone to teach me, discipline me, and look out for me when I needed it most. And in the next split second, all of that was torn from me when I heard the unmistakable sound of a crossbow shot. He died in our embrace, murdered by a cowardly goblin.

-Ven Devar

It was midnight now, and by Ven's estimation of the calm night, they would make the other side of the lake by tomorrow's sunset. Faenla and Athvar were curled up in a pile of rope while Agan slept soundly upright, back against the hull. Ven and Scáth sat at the helm, steering the gliding vessel through relatively still waters granted by the peace of night. She leaned in close, as she did so often of late, to rest her head on his shoulder. Ven leaned his head against hers, finding great nourishment in such a simple act of affection.

"I never truly thought I'd be this close to home again." Her voice was quiet and delicate. Ven said nothing. Instead, he nuzzled his head against hers in response. "Did you?" she asked while raising her head to meet his opalescent green eyes. Her luminous, stormy grey orbs never failed to disarm him. He wanted nothing but to spill his heart to her every time she looked at him.

"I think one day at a time."

She looked at him accusingly. "You're always five steps ahead of everyone," she called him out, and the Kyst sighed heavily, looking out over the open water.

"No. I did not think we would make it this far," he explained, unable to look at her. "I fear though we may be close to our goal, the dawn of something evil is nigh."

"Why did you agree to take me home?" she demanded. Ven was slightly caught off guard by her tone and pulled away from the ShadowScorn.

"Well, I mean... no one else was going to." Ven stumbled over his words and immediately regretted the ones he chose. She threw her back against the stern and crossed her arms. "That's not what I meant," he quickly said, trying to mend the situation.

"Then what did you mean?" she asked sharply. Ven looked at her with pain in his eyes. He slowly began to explain his relationship with Renic and their final moments.

"I've never truly belonged anywhere or with anyone. The good-natured Kyst of Silva gave me everything I needed to succeed, yet, I never saw myself as one with the community. I thought by fighting the Hoarfrost, I would finally feel a part of those around me; if I failed, I wouldn't be around anymore to feel anything. Of course the level of fame it brought me made that impossible. Suddenly, everyone either wanted to worship me or prove their worth against me. When I found you and saw how undeniably alone you were, I was instantly struck with a sense of relatability. Loneliness torments the mind and soul like few others. It was clear you needed to be reunited with those you belong beside. I promised myself I would see you safely home, even if it was the last thing I ever did." Tears streaked his face as he spoke, his voice never quavering. She leaned in close again, placing her head on his shoulder. She grabbed his left arm and held it close to her.

"Thank you for telling me."

He rubbed his cheek atop her wool hood. "Are you excited for what awaits you back in ShadowScorn?" From her pause, Ven could tell Scáth was hesitant to answer.

"You know by now I am the Princess of ShadowScorn?" she asked aloud. Ven just nodded, eagerly listening. "I am fourth generation. My great grandfather saw the shadowy figure in the town square that night. Now, my father and king, Arwr, has fallen ill and many plot to usurp his throne. My abduction was not random but a strategic attack from someone wanting my family gone. I do not know even now if my father is alive, but I must warn as many as possible about the impending attack." Scáth was breathing heavily now. The Kyst could feel her grip on his arm tighten as her intensity mounted.

"Upon our arrival, if I may be of any assistance, it would be my honour," the hunter offered with reverence. Although Ven could not see it under her hood, Scáth was smiling wide.

"I know," the ShadowScorn said warmly. Soon after, the Scorn found shut-eye, and Ven remained awake. The vessel was small enough to require only a single person for total operation. During the late eve, a large cloud of fog wisped together from a thin layer of mist clinging to the surface of the lake. Ven immediately caught it off the forward portside but did not understand how to respond. He gently manoeuvred the sailboat at a safe distance around the fog. The whole cloud was illuminating a faint cyan colour, and he could have sworn he saw movement from inside. Eventually, after sailing around the cloud for nearly thirty minutes, it dispersed in a small area. With mist and fog swirling around in a frenzy, he spotted a tall naked woman standing in the centre. Despite the rushing mist around her, he could tell her back was facing him. She turned one eye over her shoulder to regard the handsome Kyst. She seductively tilted her shoulder up and motioned with her finger for Ven to join her. He was so mesmerized by the way the fog danced around her body, accenting her shapely figure. Her turquoise skin twinkled as water droplets trickled down her back. She had to be the most beautiful creature in Litore, of that, the Kyst was sure. He felt himself gripping the taffrail and slowly leaning over.

"Grrrrr." Faenla's growl reverberated maliciously toward Ven. The hunter reacted so genuinely to the growl he caught himself on his back foot with one hand on his short sword hilt. At that sight, the majestic Faenla snorted and dropped his head back down on his front paws. Ven looked back to the cloud to see the woman was no longer in sight, he felt ridiculous and confused. Kyst, like many elves in Litore, are impervious to the magic of the mind. He thought perhaps, the longer he stayed awake the easier it was for such magics to permeate his thoughts. He woke Agan, who was glad to take over for the hunter. The fighter was used to taking shifts during the night and was relieved when Ven finally found rest.

Agan spotted land in the distance as dawn had backlit the sky. The other adventurers awoke to oddly warm air, a sunny sky, and a shared sense of optimism. They collectively agreed to ditch the boat in a thicket of weeds as opposed to docking anywhere that could draw attention to themselves or possibly have more Sesaran soldiers waiting. Faenla was first off the boat; he unintentionally amazed everyone by leaping several metres to land on solid ground. Ven tied the sailboat to a fallen tree nearby for the next lucky traveller or resident of the lake.

From there, they travelled southeast through more valleys and small rivers that spread like roots off of Litore Lake. Walking along a ridgeline near the top of one valley edge, Ven led the group with Agan behind him.

"Has much returned to you?" Ven questioned Agan about this every other day it seemed.

"I'm afraid not," the half-orc replied, rather disgruntled with himself.

"I did not know you were of the Sesara faith," Ven pointed out, not in judgment but as something new he had learned about the mysterious wanderer. Agan laughed aloud as his hand grabbed several different coloured chains from around his neck and out under his armour. Ven turned to regard what was so funny, and upon doing so, the Kyst did join in on the laugh. For Agan was holding pendants, each linked to a different coloured chain of at least six deities. Sesara was on a gold chain, Skalgr the Diamond Dragon on a red chain. Aceia, God of Shadow and Assassins was connected to a matt black chain. Even the symbol for Ven's supposed Gods, Kaia and Āina, were connected to a bright blue and brown chain. He noted a few other chains of varying colours. Ven turned forward again with a large smile on his face as he continued to navigate the cliffside path.

They broke for camp still high on the west side of a valley known as Risastor Gorge after Scáth's great grandfather. She told them a tale of how he heroically led the new people of ShadowScorn against an impromptu attack from Renrit, a large region of devout Sesaran followers. After devouring a well-earned meal that night, they all noticed a small glow of concentrated lights coming from the Highlands southwest of them.

"Do you think that's them?" Scáth said aloud to anyone willing to answer. Athvar, ever the optimist, answered the worried ShadowScorn.

"I'm sure it's a small village, or perhaps even a convoy travelling along the road." He tried his hardest to reassure Scáth, though he never felt as if he did a good enough job in that regard. Everyone found rest that night, safely tucked along the ridge, out of reach from harm's way. The next evening brought an exhalation of joy when the adventures broke for camp in view of the great lone, Glass Mountain in which ShadowScorn is built along its eastern base. Yet come darkness, they spotted the same glow but nearly half again as close to them.

"What were you saying last night, little man?" Agan asked Athvar in a mocking tone. The gnome just rolled his big eyes and looked out over the vista. It was all too real for Scáth now, it was obvious the church of Sesara meant war, and the large army from Renrit marched on her home even now. They were too far away to get the size of the approaching army, only truly distinguishable from the thousands upon thousands of torches dimly brightening the sky around them. Truthfully, Ven could not say he was surprised by the unfolding events. Once it became clear Scáth was no ordinary Scorn, and her abduction was in an attempt of political gain, it all made sense. The Kyst knew enough of Litore's history to know that man will always call to war, especially under the banner of a higher power. He considered it was possible humans rushed to fight given they were one of the shorter-lived races on Litore. Yet, he did admit to himself that it was far more than he ever expected when starting this quest. Ven Devar was firmly confident in his and his companion's ability to do whatever was necessary to protect those in need. He placed his hand on Scáth's shoulder, she turned to regard him, and when she did, she found a smile that comforted her unlike ever before. Scáth felt a sense of safety when in the company of her companions that she was not familiar with. Not even when the royal ScornGuard was around for her protection growing up. She was glad to be going into the current circumstances with friends like these by her side. They had become a cohesive team in the previous months and found even greater strength with the addition of Agan Dusk.

CHAPTER SEVENTEEN
Revenge

The flames vividly outlined the cloaked silhouette of Rexous, watching the small fishing village of nearly one-hundred Kyst turn to ash. The night was dark, and nearly thirty Kintar anxiously awaited their leader's next command. Rexous stared into the fires of that so recently peaceful village. The bodies of the inhabitants were strewn about, wherever they were savagely struck down. In the recent weeks, Rexous and his band of Kintar had slaughtered and burned nearly two thousand Kyst and their homes. Always leaving a few victims to spread the word of the betrayer Ven Devar and the atrocities committed against his people. Uthul strode up behind Rexous, and gave him a fair distance of space. Not out of respect but for fear of Rexous simply turning on him in this moment of brutality.

"It is time. The wizard has come for us," Uthul said loudly over the sound of roaring flames. All was still for a moment before Rexous slowly turned and approached Uthul.

"Then let us go," he offered with particular dryness in his voice. Uthul wasted no time in leading the way toward the wizard from Serenstrom. First, Uthul told one of the few actual ranking Kintar to take the raiding party back to Claw Canyon where they could expect a pile of riches for a job well done. The duo of Kyst found the wizard waiting on a Seacliff above the burning village. They saw him finishing an incantation, then gingerly looking over the edge of the cliff before facing them with a grin.

"Good evening," the wizard greeted with respect.

"How will we be joining your army from here?" Rexous asked doubtfully. The wizard simply motioned over the edge of the cliff, a near 600-metre drop to the jagged stones and crashing waves below. Uthul raised his brow as the two Kyst looked over the edge to see a small yellow swirling portal. From way up here, it looked to be only a short distance above the white-capped waves.

"You cannot be serious," Uthul blurted unpleased.

"This particular spell requires a certain amount of speed before entering the portal. You are asking me to send you thousands of kilometres away. This is what it will take." And with that, the wizard crossed his arms on his chest and fell back first off the cliff, straight through his portal. Uthul looked wide-eyed at Rexous, who shrugged in return and put one foot over the edge. He leaned forward, not wanting to give it much thought and jumped. It was exhilarating as the mist from the coast pelted his face on the descent. It took nearly twelve seconds to fall the distance, but it felt far longer than that. He shot through the portal with immense speed and came skidding out the other side through a field of tall grass. Rexous got to his hands and knees, fighting the overwhelming urge to vomit, digging his fingernails into the dirt to fight the vertigo. He heard a large suction sound and saw Uthul catch the ground with his shoulder and go flying into the air in a summersault. The wizard walked over to Rexous, offering him aid, but Rex slapped his hand away. So the wizard offered the same to Uthul, who was happy for the assistance. Rex looked around in amazement at his surroundings. He had travelled some of Litore with his mother but never this far east. He saw Glass Mountain painted against the vast, star-filled sky. Not so far in the distance, the white canvas tents and the glow of torches could be seen from the Renrit army approaching from the west. The former prince joined the now recovered 'Betrayer.'

"As promised. ShadowScorn is but a day's walk," the wizard spoke proudly, for he was quite happy with how his spell of teleportation had gone.

"Good," was all the Kyst said before throwing a dagger in the neck of the magician. With the flick of his other hand, he released a dagger to embed in Uthul's spine. Rexous watched as the wizard dropped and began drowning from his own blood flooding his lungs. He then bent over Uthul and watched him suffer for a moment.

"Your mistake was thinking me a mere pawn. I know you killed my mother, and unlike you, she did not keep secrets from me." Uthul could not have looked stunned if he wanted to, for the dagger perfectly severed his spinal cord. Blood poured from his mouth and had begun to fill the Kyst's eyes, tainting his vision red. "I know who you really are, father. I've prayed every night since the fire that whatever awaits you in the afterlife is a never-ending torment," Rexous said with a haunting tone of finality. Uthul eventually sucked his last gulp of air, and the Kyst walked away from the scene as emotionally detached from his actions as ever.

The adventurers got to an early start the next day, rising before the day's first light. They kept a speedy pace in hopes of closing the distance to ShadowScorn as quickly as possible. They knew that by the end of this day, the approaching army would have found suitable ground to fortify. The group never lost sight of them, for the route Scáth had chosen as the quickest and safest took them on a kilometre high path along Glass Mountain. By dusk's fading light, the trail would lead them to a secret entrance into the city. Athvar found great ease in traversing the thin mountain path. However, Agan and Faenla found it to be a delicate one step at a time scenario. It was rarely wider than thirty centimetres, with loose pebbles creating a less than smooth path. In several places the route was gone altogether, having been taken out in rockslides past. The sky was a bright gold, and it warmed the face of the mountain with surprising heat. The group could see the Renrit army setting up their camp roughly a kilometre or two from the base of the mountain.

"We're two hours from the city wall," Scáth excitedly declared to the group. It warmed everyone's heart to finally see her in such high spirits, though it was obvious she had pressing concerns on her mind. Ven felt a sense of friendship between his companions he had never known before. Not even among the hunters of Silva did the orphan Kyst feel truly accepted or akin to those around him. He always knew he had never truly fit in as a Kyst, culturally, finding most of their traditions to be unsatisfying to his very core. When he was beside Faenla, the two apex predators felt as though they could defeat any foe. When he was walking with Athvar 'the Undusted', he was always reminded of how special and important their connection to nature really was. The gnome had taught Ven a great many things regarding communication and animal behaviours but also helped him with the wisdom of a full life lived, as a mentor might. Agan, who had joined the group halfway, fit in as well as anyone. He was a formidable warrior with elven grace and orcish strength. Scáth, above all else, made Ven believe in what they were doing. She opened his eyes to the fact that everything he ever sought in life was possible. She proved to him that a sense of belonging was attainable for the Mighty Kyst hunter. She questioned him when she knew he was wrong and encouraged him when she knew he was right. Ven was truly thankful for such a wise and caring soul to have entered his life. He promised himself but already knew in his heart, he would do whatever it took to keep each one of them safe.

Nearly an hour out of the city walls, Scáth halted the group for a small rockslide had just begun ahead of them. Once the rumble settled, they proceeded forward until they came to a ninety-degree bend in the path. Scáth went around first and disappeared out of sight.

"I really hate this," Agan muttered under his breath as he watched Ven go around the corner. The wind picked up just as he breached the severe bend in the mountain face, causing his cloak to billow out wildly. When he looked up toward Scáth, she was facing him with a single hand pressed to her mouth and a dagger held tightly to her throat. Ven's heart skipped a beat as if he had just seen a ghost. He never expected to see Rexous again and certainly not dressed exactly as he was on the side of a mountain halfway across the world.

"Let her go!" Ven yelled at the once prince and rival elf. Rexous continued to hold Scáth aggressively, now with a smirk on his face. Wondering what the yelling was about, Athvar poked his head around the corner and briskly pulled himself back, pressing his little body firmly against the mountain face.

"What is it?" Agan shouted over the speeding wind.

"Another Kyst!" Athvar replied as loudly as his small voice could. Agan gave the gnome a confused look, and they both noticed Faenla standing between them, beginning to rile up.

"What do you want, Rex?" Ven asked with a fierce anger.

"I want to avenge my home, my former life. Everything you took from me." Rexous spat with intense malice.

"I had nothing to do with any of it. It was Uthul, Rexous! I loved your mother. You know that more than anyone." Ven slowly raised one hand out toward Scáth, who reciprocated the gesture. "Please don't shed more innocent blood, release her."

Rexous looked tired. After weeks of constant battle, he wasn't himself. His emotions dictated his actions and were completely unchecked by judgment. Ven could tell he was in great anguish simply by the scowl that never seemed to leave his face. After a tense moment of Rexous staring into Ven's soul, he loosened his grip and let the ShadowScorn free. She nimbly manoeuvred around to be behind Ven.

"I know everything that happened with far greater clarity than even you. I've already killed Uthul. And once I've killed you, I'll end that foolish Macer." Rexous threw a dagger with lightning speed, but Ven deflected it, ricocheting off his bracer. He immediately came in at Ven with his free hand across his chest, swinging a dagger reverse grip. Ven pushed his back to the mountain, catching the extended arm with both hands. Ven snapped his hand, and the dagger fell free from Rexous. He then spun them around to shove Rexous' face hard into the stone. The once prince gave a great grunt of pain as his cheekbone cracked against the rock. Scáth couldn't believe the display of martial combat with such minimal space around them, but they were Kyst after all.

Rexous slid his foot in front of Ven's leg and kicked back as hard as he could. Ven's leg gave way, and his foot slipped off the narrow edge. Rexous pushed against the rock face with all his force, causing Ven to fully slip backwards off the mountainside. As the hunter's lower body fell clean from the path, Ven grabbed the well-planted ankle of Rexous. He didn't have to pull hard, for his falling weight was all it took to pull Rexous down with him. Rex smashed his forehead against the stone, skinning his shins on the mountain edge before tumbling down with his sworn enemy.

Scáth let out a gut-wrenching scream as she threw herself to her belly, one hand extended down toward Ven. She helplessly watched as they tumbled over each other, plummeting down the side of the mountain. She saw Ven connect squarely with large boulders three separate times before losing sight of both Kyst in a thicket of trees nearly a hundred metres down. Faenla nimbly leaped over Athvar and came around the harsh bend as quickly as possible to see Scáth on her belly, sobbing helplessly. Faenla gave a long melancholic howl of defiance as he began gingerly trying to put his first paw over the steep edge. Scáth threw herself on top of Faenla, tears carving streaks through dirt-covered cheeks.

"Don't! Don't leave me, Faen." The ShadowScorn buried her face in the alpha's thick coat of fur. Athvar and Agan made it around the corner to witness the defeated Scáth and Faenla. Athvar leaned over the edge straining his vision for any sign of life, any sign that Ven may have survived. Agan stood against the mountain face, stunned at the realization before the soldier in him took over.

"The sun will set soon. We must be off this mountainside come dark," he said solemnly. Scáth pulled away from the wolf to stare at Agan with intense hate-filled eyes.

"I will personally come out and look for him, Scáth. We cannot fail to have you inside your city walls without delay," he said authoritatively. Agan didn't like it any more than anyone else, but it could not be more simple. They would not last the night on that thin path, and it was clear now they could be found by the enemy. Scáth looked to Athvar, who was getting back up to his stubby and sturdy legs.

"He's right, Lady Scáth. We will come back with help as soon as possible, of that, I promise ya," he offered softly to the nearly inconsolable Scorn as he placed his small and delicate hand on hers. Like a nightmare she could not wake up from, Scáth stood up and continued along the mountain trail that now sloped down toward the great City of Shadow. The group was quiet, except for Faenla, who, despite the pleas of his companions, continued to howl in distress. Upon reaching a large rock wall at the end of their trail, Scáth halted the group.

"Wait here a moment. I wish not to alarm the guard," Scáth instructed her friends as she approached a small stone door, barely noticeable against the rock wall. She gave a series of knocks that elicited a small stone vidette to open. They noticed Scáth lower the hood on her cloak, and the door immediately flung open for her. She waved for her companions to follow, and with that, the group entered the high-walled city of ShadowScorn.

CHAPTER EIGHTEEN
Ven Devar

Ven knew in the first split second his foot went over the edge that it was all or nothing. If he truly wanted to keep his promise to Scáth, he would have to pull Rexous down with him. He understood the sacrifice was necessary and accepted it as his destiny. Firmly grasping Rexous and dropping his weight, the two Kyst rolled and tumbled, ricocheting off boulders, skin grating against loose shale and coarse stone. Ven was completely unaware of how far they had fallen, dazed by the unfathomable amount of blunt force trauma. Every time he bounced upwards, he thought for sure he'd be flung off the mountainside, only to splat against the rocky basin below. Eventually, the pair did soar off a sheer drop of twelve metres before Ven hit a tree of equal height, falling and landing on a bent and twisted knee. He felt a crack, heard a pop and screamed as loud as he ever had, but nothing escaped his lungs. Then blackness consumed his vision, dropping his unconscious head to the snowy stone.

Rexous had his foot jammed between a rock and a thick root, but the momentum of his fall tore him free, dislocating his ankle, left to hang there by muscle and tendons. He rolled down the sparsely-grass-covered rock until his jaw collided with the trunk of a black birch tree. Several teeth shot forth, knocking the Kyst senseless. Although they did not know it, they had landed only thirty metres from each other. Rexous had flown further down the mountain, landing near the bottom of the trees where it ended in a 500-metre drop. Both Kyst lay battered and bruised, pulled deep into their subconsciousness, safely away from the agonizing torment of their bodies.

The darkness of night blanketed them, and a frigid air whistled across the mountain. Rexous was awoken by the brilliant light of the moons dancing in the reflection of the snow. He rolled onto his back and sat up, wincing from a sudden shock of pain pulsating from his ankle up his leg. He took a deep breath when he saw his heel where his toes should be, now realizing the full extent of his injury. He continued to breathe deeply, but it quickly became coarse and aggravated as he hoisted himself up, using the trident for support. His left eye was swollen and sealed shut by dried blood. He could feel multiple pieces of flapping torn flesh soaking his tunic. Nevertheless, he determinedly looked around the small plateau he landed on but found no sign of his sworn enemy.

Ven woke up in fright, drenched with sweat and chilled blood. His dislocated knee tormented his body with searing agony. He closed his eyes tightly, grabbed his knee with both hands and tugged and twisted with all his might until a loud familiar popping sound was heard. He couldn't help but let out a screech of pain as he fell back, staring up at the stars through the sparse tree canopy. His eyes brimmed heavy with tears, both from pain and sorrow. Rexous clearly heard where the yelp of pain had come from, and so he hobbled his way there. Soon, they spotted each other, equally bruised and broken. Ven had received a large gash across his forehead down his right eye from a jagged piece of stone. He couldn't be sure until a healer had their inspection, but it felt as though his collar bone was fractured and pushing out against his armour. Judging by the movement of Rexous, though, Ven felt confident his counterpart had suffered equally.

"I don't understand," Ven stammered, getting to his feet, using the tree he collided with as support and removing a dagger from his greave as he stood. "Why didn't you return to us and just claim your seat as king?" He ended up leaning his good shoulder against the tree.

"I am forever changed by the flames that scarred our world," Rexous said honestly while removing a dagger sheathed above his hip. He stood battered and heavily leaning on his trident for support, barely able to keep his enemy in focus.

Ven understood he was suffering from a concussion but thought Rex was wearing his clothes. "Why are you dressed as I?" he asked, slightly swaying back and forth from blood loss. Rexous managed to form a smirk through all the pain.

"By now, the whole Northern Rainforest knows the 'Mighty Ven Devar' to be nothing more than a Kyst killing traitor." The once prince spat a mouth full of blood at Ven, launching his dagger. Ven saw the ploy for what it was and threw his dagger with equal speed. The hunters both saw their daggers find their mark, and they both heard the sound of steel piercing their own flesh. Almost as if in sync, they looked down to their chests, where they both then grasped at the blade hilt protruding from their armour.

"What have you done?" Ven asked in shock while looking at the weapon embedded in his lower right breast. Rexous looked up from the dagger to the Kyst he had grown up with.

"I finally killed you," Rexous answered with fading anguish. Tears brimmed his one good eye as he stared down the 'Mighty Ven Devar'. Before the famed hunter could respond, the Prince of Silva fell to the blood-soaked snow, utterly lifeless. Ven exhaled sharply as the blade collapsed his lung. He slumped down the tree, legs sprawled out in front of him. He gasped intensely from grabbing the hilt of the dagger, the slight movement of the blade causing more blood to flow freely. He sat there looking at Rexous, grief and misery washing over him like a hot sickness. He caught himself fighting the urge to fall unconscious, his head plunging forward before lazily snapping it back up. The swell of emotion and physical torment became too much for the Mighty Hunter. Resisting proved to make things worse, and before long, the Kyst's head bobbed forward one last time, eyes shut tight.

A small dinghy floating atop the rough sea rises and falls with the great rolling waves. With no shoreline in sight and no apparent passengers, a lone Kyst baby lay swaddled in cloth on the hull floor. Crying profusely, scared, and alone. A loud reverberation echoes through the hull of the dinghy, and the poor Kyst baby begins crying even louder. Soon the babe quiets, as a young and slender Kyst hunter, dressed for fishing leaps aboard. The hunter picks the child up with tender care, the baby quietly cooing now, mesmerized by its saviour staring back at him. Ven re-lived the dream, as he had his whole life.

The Kyst slowly opened his eyes, and for the first time, without fear. This new revelation was enforced when he saw Faenla, Athvar, and Agan sitting around a fire on the opposite wall of his bed's footboard. Scáth, who had been sitting beside him since the night before, looked at him with the watery eyes of elation. A smile he never thought he'd be fortunate enough to see again.

"Milady." Before he finished speaking the words, Scáth had her arms wrapped around his neck in a loving embrace. He had a hard time lifting his arms, but soon he was returning the hug best he could. They were interrupted when Faenla had stuck his large snout under their arms, breaking them apart so he could repetitively lick Ven's face. The Kyst accepted the kisses from his wolf companion with excitement and quickly pulled their foreheads together. Re-sharing that special moment when the three of them stumbled upon each other in the forest that one fateful night.

"Yar lucky to be alive, Ven!" Athvar leaped up onto the bed and walked right up to the hunter, making them the same eye level, which was a novelty for both. "Just a smidge to the left and yad'a been a goner!" Athvar said, poking Ven in the bandaged chest, right next to where the dagger had struck.

"How did you get me?" Ven asked curiously.

"Scáth immediately sent us back out with a healer and climbing gear. We had you in here before sunrise," Agan said casually as if the entire procedure of retrieving Ven wasn't at all hazardous or complicated. Ven just smiled at the half-elf before being swept back to reality.

"Where is Rexous?" he hastily inquired with some degree of discomfort. Athvar and Agan avoided eye contact, leaving Ven to look to Scáth for answers.

"Athvar is right, whether it be luck or destiny. Our clerics could heal the wound he dealt you. Yet, your dagger strike killed him hours before we got there." Scáth knew Ven would be bothered by the death of Rexous, especially by his hand, so she offered her words empathetically. "What matters now is we're all okay. You fulfilled your promise to me. There are those who wish to meet the legendary 'Mighty Ven Devar'. The Kyst hunter that saw me safely home," she said with a renewed sense of optimism.

"Don't forget we're at war too!" Athvar chimed in sarcastically, as usual, to which everyone shot him disappointed looks for dampening the joyous moment.

"Of course. But, might we all... remain here awhile first?" Ven asked with a vulnerability unseen by any of his companions before. For Ven Devar awoke unafraid for the first time in his life, understanding that even if just for now, he found a place and group wherein he felt true belonging. With that, Scáth slid next to the Kyst pulling him close to her side and tousling his thick forest green hair back. Faenla sat neatly close to Ven where he could offer licks unhindered. Athvar jumped and landed on the bed butt first, legs crossed and gave a bellowing laugh. Agan sat in a large fur-lined chair, offering the group a flask he manifested from seemingly nowhere. They shared a collective laugh of merriment and began recounting their many harrowing adventurers.